Victim's Vengeance

By Kenneth M. Lee

Printed in the United States of America

Victim's Vengeance, by Kenneth M. Lee

This is a work of fiction, though similar stories like this have happened in the country in the last century, with the inordinate amount of technology and evil people in the world.

Names, characters, places, and incidences are purely the works of imagination, though a few of the physical locations in the Tidewater area are real. But any resemblance to actual persons, living or dead, businesses, companies, and events, are purely coincidental.

Library of Congress Control Number 2022910494

ISBN 9780971185067

Kenneth Lee has two other books available at Amazon: *God's Divine Help* and *Persecuted But Not Forsaken*

Victim's Vengeance

By Kenneth M. Lee

To Regina

Always Faithful

1.

Zenithe Organization was spread around the globe with a surveillance system, stalker cells, and people in management positions in governments and private industry.

The organization relied mainly on technology to get their way – manipulating the marketplace and harnessing offenders of their programs.

Their electronic weapons system piggy-backed off cell phone towers and microwave repeaters, and it could target anyone anywhere.

But one thing Zenithe's organizers had not abandoned from its archaic beginning was using people on the ground to identify and stalk targets.

The organization's by-laws that had originated from the beginning of civilization always worked. Deception, manipulation, spying, and sometimes using force over the people had always kept the organization secure and profitable in the world.

Now, here in the year 2022, with their long term goal of placing personnel in key American Government positions achieved, it was only a matter of time before citizens of every nation would be enslaved and totally controlled to perform whatever mission desired. The organization would use the Americans and technology to accomplish the goal.

It had been fun for the leaders of Zenithe in the last decade; there were no threatening adversaries to their mission, but governments were beginning to employ computer forensic specialists and threatening to blow up anyone trespassing on designated parts of the electromagnetic wave spectrum.

Oh, it was so lucrative to use the victims for sexual acts and sell them to the dark part of the Internet. And if the victims committed suicide, their body parts would be hurriedly extracted and sold for medicines, food, and research.

But now there was confusion; hackers were getting into the control programs and investigators were swarming the airwaves.

"There are communication towers in every town," Rulemin exclaimed to his partners. "Do not worry. We control people, judges, and the jury!"

His talk did nothing to calm the worried faces of the other three men who were also sitting in the Switzerland condo on the side of a mountain smoking Dominican importantly judges, politicians, juries, police, prisoners, and especially the governors of each state and their staff. No one would be excluded, especially Department of Justice and Defense employees who had the know-how to find the organization.

There were over 4000 main victims now scattered around the world. 500 were in the United States.

The computers would trigger an alert when a victim came close to exposing their operation, and two men would evaluate the problem and take action to hinder or eliminate the problem -- but rule number one was to never become directly involved in a malady or death of a targeted victim. Remoteness was the key for safety and security.

Eventually the system would target everyone on earth but the operators, who had secret locations in radio free zones in idyllic places. No other person on earth would be able to escape the electro-magnetic field bondage.

Steal their money, have their children raped, and occupy their houses – free – with no chance of getting prosecuted – as long as the test victims and the future populace were kept under control.

But one victim was different; as Marcia Lane Lemay looked at her computer monitor thousands of miles away in Newport News, Virginia, at an Internet address that told her she was being tracked and targeted from a location somewhere near Australia.

Marcia was an investigator in her own right, but not by choice. She was a former paralegal that contracted out services to law firms on a semi-yearly basis until she found herself in front of a legal case that had all the marks of a firm representing a client in a worker's compensation case yet being party to causing the client's disability with covert targeting.

She decided to look for another job, but the job never left her.

Now there was an alert on her computer that someone was monitoring her.

3.

"Is she implanted?" computer analyst Tori asked from the organization's electronic monitoring room in the Bougainville mine shaft.

The shaft was surrounded by thick jungle growth and tall trees on the south side of a hill. It was a perfect place to intercept private and National Security Agency communications from New Zealand and around the world because of its height and proximity to overhead satellites, antennas, and microwave communications towers. A considerable amount of Internet traffic had been diverted to this small island and mine shaft.

"No. And that's a problem," Brahaim responded.

Brahaim was an associate who acted in liaison with ground personnel in the U.S. who provided visual identification of victims. He knew if victims had drugged foods, implant composites, or micro-chips in them that could be activated by direct targeting or electromagnetic energies from cell phone towers and the 60 Hertz electrical grid transformers.

He was responsible for all North American covert activities including Canada and Mexico.

"We can manipulate her movements and actions but not always her thoughts and words. Maybe no oral drug composites exist in her throat. I don't know!"

Tori looked at other monitors showing images of victims. *What if they are trying to fool us with heated dummies,* he thought, as his mind was wandering and thinking about infrared energy. The victims had been getting smarter as time went on.

The workstation got to him sometimes, but the money was good. In a few more months, because of his one year stay here in the bunker, he would be receiving a bonus of $50,000.

But seeing innocent people being targeted to lose their assets, emotions, and sometimes their body parts -- well, it was beginning to get to him, and the same thing could happen to him if he left the organization prematurely.

At 35 years old he had to do something, because former jobs like soliciting condo time share agreements and installing new computer software for accounting firms were not paying the bills.

After a brief chat with a friend about the money that could be made keeping people under surveillance, he found himself on this island entering numbered codes into computers for individual citizens at the end of each day in this dark bunker.

Distracted, he looked out the one small window near the door entrance and saw thick black clouds forming over the ocean and waves of water reaching 8 feet.

Tori looked back at the monitor trying to shake himself of the storm image but hanging onto an image of freedom: he would be lying on the beach in a faraway country and not this hidden hellhole of evil trying to control humanity.

The third man in the bunker, who was called "Premiere", suddenly appeared aware of the victim problem.

He was called Premiere because he was first in command of this center and got directions straight from the family in Switzerland.

He gave an order, "Engage the infrared scope from Sat24 which should be crossing nearby. Get her coordinates and apply a search beam for two seconds in a 5' circle. Don't hurt her. Just get her out of that room away from the computer."

4.

Tori walked over to the Sat24 computer link and hoped the storm had done nothing to rip the antenna off the tree outside and typed in instructions with a code for the IR to be engaged around the circumference of the targeting coordinates at 35th Street, Building B, Apartment 2, at the west bedroom of Marcia's apartment in Newport News, Virginia.

If Marcia did not move in the next five minutes to exit the room, then a different energy would be delivered.

Tori hated to see it done because victims often got burned and it took days for them to recover.

Tori went back to the monitor and watched.

Brahaim, the second in command, spoke up. "If she gets to that computer again and calls her lawyer boyfriend about her suspicions of Jon Skooly, we're cooked, and Cell 1 will go down."

The old man, Jon Skooly, was an attorney who had an office in Hampton, Virginia with three other attorneys where Marcia had worked as a paralegal for several months.

On the dark side, Skooly was commandeering ground stalking and surveillance for Cell 1, which covered the eastern part of Virginia north of the James River to Washington D.C. It had a command center in Newport News where there was a hot bed of activity of international shipping at the port, discarded military supplies at nearby Fort Eustis, and intelligence agencies throughout the area where paid off informants would pick up on any suspect surveillance from the feds.

Cell 1 was important not only because of a logistical place in the middle of the East Coast of America, but with communications access to Washington D.C. and Langley A.F.B. where moles had been placed in the C.I.A. and F.B.I. Further, nearby Congressional politicians could be influenced to introduce legislative bills that favored Zenithe -- like less restrictions at ship off loading platforms and highway weighing stations.

Cell 1 operated out of River Business Center on James River Highway. Skooly's office was five miles away near Hampton Institute where he could solicit college students into doing some of his dirty work, like following victims around, making noise, or sabotaging a victim's belongings.

It was in Skooly's office Marcia accessed files that linked Skooly to a group of professional gangsters that were targeting Skooly's clients by drugging, stalking, and stealing bank cards, cash, and valuables.

Worse, Marcia found evidence technicians were being used to canvas a person's home remotely with surveillance energy and used mind control equipment to get victims labeled as schizophrenic and into a psychiatric hospital.

Centrex Company was a local player who furnished high tech gadgetry to harass and oppress people with mind control programs. The company was located just outside of town in a supposedly empty warehouse along the James River, where they would receive goods along with drugs from boat or vehicle. Here, on the river, they could send Morse code messages to drug boats travelling the river and never be on tower communication links.

Marcia was sitting at her computer in a bathrobe and felt the burning first starting at the top of her head and then along her shoulders.

She hurriedly saved the IP number on the screen and turned off the computer. She unplugged the power cord and threw a piece of foil with black plastic over the screen and left the room.

At 5' 8" tall, 112 pounds, with blond hair, narrow shoulders and a slim face, she drew men's attention, but she didn't want this kind of attention she was getting from some kind of loony who was on the other end of a computer and using high tech equipment to try and kill her.

She had never reported Skooly's illegal operation to law enforcement -- just left a notice of retiring the contract due to unforeseen and negative circumstances.

But these people are highly paranoid from their illegal activities and they snoop around on anyone they think might tell, she thought.

Lord knows she was prepared for this encounter by growing up with two brothers who thrived on competitive challenges; Marcia found herself in the furor of heated ball games, board game competitions, and physical endurance activities trying to keep up with them.

But this was different, because someone was out to hurt her, and they had high tech equipment monitoring her every move.

She sat on a couch in the living room recovering from the burning and thinking about what to do.

Maybe she could spend some time at her boyfriend Richie's place. Maybe she could just stay away from the computer and go about her business.

All these thoughts ran through her mind as she wiped her face with a wet wash cloth. She brushed her shoulder length blonde hair back to feel air on her ears.

She got up and went to the laundry room to get a tan jersey knit shirt, brown jogging pants, and a pair of tennis shoes, just in case she had to run.

Normally, she's let her hair just hang down, but today she would draw it up and tie it off with a dark blue ribbon behind her head to look different. Any advantage she could get against her stalker might save her life.

She lacquered her lips with an antique silver lipstick.

Girly is what she wanted. If she was going to be an investigator and someone different, she might as well have fun doing it.

She would lock the apartment door and get in the car and think some more about what to do. There, in the car's metal enclosure, she would be able to think a little and be somewhat safe.

She disabled her cell phone by taking out the battery.

She had to leave, but first she would hide her foods and valuables, stuff some supplements in her purse, and get two razor blades to tape underside the front door knob just in case someone tried to enter. Who else would go to the trouble of turning the door knob but her stalker?

She pulled the door shut while sticking a marker at the jamb and taped the blades under the knob. She walked down the steps to the parking lot.

Marcia triggered a light beam which had been covertly installed by one ex-convict Julian Muestro, who lived in an apartment across the street. He wanted to know when anyone came or went from the apartment. The beam disruption sent an audible wireless signal to his computer.

Out of the corner of her eye as she opened the door of the car, she saw a curtain suddenly close in a second story apartment window.

But maybe she was just being overly paranoid.

5.

Julian Muestro was being blackmailed by Skooly to watch Marcia. He remembered the day well.

"You're getting 3 years for breaking and entering Bobby's Texaco Jules," Skooly had said as the two men lingered on a red brick pavement sidewalk outside the swinging door entrance to the Circuit Court minutes before a sentencing hearing by Judge Farrow.

Skooly nodded to other lawyers who were entering the doors and let that statement sink into Julian before saying anything else.

"I can't do that. I got a wife and kid. I need help!" Jules responded.

Skooly thought Julian wasn't ready to submit to an alternative plan so he began to walk from the court lobby area to the court room. Julian nervously followed him to a bench just outside Courtroom #2.

The waiting area was quiet as this was the only contested case scheduled at this time in the morning for Judge Farrow.

Skooly obviously knew the outcome of the sentencing. He had worked with Farrow for years and the two men had recently discussed this case over breakfast.

Finally, Julian with shaking hands and nervous chatter spoke up, "Is there any way you can get this sentence reduced?"

Skooly lifted his eyebrows somewhat and said, "If you can do some work for me."

"Sure. Sure. Whatever. What is it? I don't kill people, okay? I just want to stay out of prison!"

"I might get you probation for three years with community service since this is a second time offense. How's that?" Skooly asked.

Julian said, "Great! What do you want me to do?"

"I want you to watch someone for me. Maybe disturb her a little."

"Yea. Yes. Sure man. Just keep me out of prison. This is great. But I don't want to hurt no one."

Skooly entered the doors of the room and gave a wink to Farrow who was already sitting behind the podium with a gavel exposed in his right hand.

Skooly gave Farrow a previously typed order for this very moment. Farrow signed it after a few vain questions and got up and left the podium area.

18

Now Julian found himself as one of Skooly's street thugs and in one of Skooly's real estate friend's apartments across the street from Marcia keeping her under surveillance.

He did not like breaking in the apartment and drugging her drinks, but every time he objected, Skooly threatened him with prison

Hearing the audible alarm, Julian put aside his newspaper and took his empty coffee cup to the kitchen. He walked over to the front window to see Marcia making her way down the sidewalk to her gold colored Honda.

She would head north on Royal Street and more than likely to her boyfriend Richie's house. She's a cute thing, he was thinking. *She will be gone for the day more than likely, and if she does come back early, the tracking device on her car will alert me.*

Julian went to the bedroom and got some dark clothing and put them out on a bed. He went to the bathroom and got some barbiturates from the medicine cabinet and put them in his black pants pocket.

In a hallway closet, he got the numbered keys for her front door deadbolt. He made sure he had an old credit card in his wallet to slip along the striker plate for the knob latch. He slid a pair of gloves in the pants pockets, and he went back to the living room to wait awhile. He thanked God he was not in prison.

6.

Marcia backed out of her parking space and went north on Oak Street, the back way, and turned north onto Route 17.

She passed another low income multi-family apartment complex with tenants loitering outside under oak and maple trees trying to get relief from the heat on this humid morning.

Kids rode their bicycles in circles, a lone cat scampered away from a couple of teenagers, and mothers looked anxiously at their young babies who were in playpens or plastic tubs filled with a couple of inches of water. One day she'd have it better and move to a better location, but for now, and being without a job, she had no choice but to rent in this low income district.

Richie's situation was different: A trial lawyer by trade, he was living in a nice condominium apartment complex overlooking a tidal creek near Williamsburg. The condo was constructed of archaic red brick, had white shutters around the windows, and slate tiles covered the roof. The lawn outside was manicured. Bermuda grass with pebbled walkways surrounded the community. It was heaven compared to her place.

But Richie was a lawyer who had a sole practice and doing quite well.

Marcia met Richie at a deposition hearing where Marcia was transcribing oral testimony of one Starr Hendricks who was suing her husband for cars, houses, stocks, bonds, and if she could get it, future interest from a perpetual family retirement fund investment.

"He just got up and left me all alone!" she exclaimed at a hearing.

"And then what did you do?" Richie had asked as her attorney sat stone faced and mesmerized by the proceedings and the story.

"I called my lawyer!"

"That fast?" responded Richie.

"Well yes! If you had been hurt and ignored and abused like what he did to me, you'd call and leave too!"

Marcia typed furiously while looking up occasionally to make sure she got every word.

Richie had a difficult time questioning Mrs. Hendricks's ramblings with the pretty blonde girl typing away and her white laced blouse occasionally rippling with an air conditioner fan blowing and her tanned arms moving with every stroke of the keyboard.

Her feet dangled as she typed and her brown sandals scraped the floor every so often. Then during a pause, she'd push her blonde hair back over her ears and stare at him, which only made it worse. The room was only 12' x 12' with no windows and it was getting hot.

"And do you have any marks to show where he abused you?" Richie continued.

"Well no. It just hurt," Hendricks continued.

Richie looked at Marcia to make sure she got that response. In unison she looked back momentarily to let him know she did.

There was an agreement there, and he wanted to pursue it farther, whether because of Mrs. Hendricks's slick answers or a desire to know Marcia better.

Four days later, when asking if the transcript was available, he talked to her on the phone and asked her out for lunch.

Marcia had been with Richie seven months now and felt comfortable enough to visit anytime as long he wasn't in the middle of a trial. She understood completely the concentration an attorney must have when filing motions, depositions, and legal briefs.

But she was having a rough time with this energy targeting, and she was scared for her life and trying not to show it.

Questions continued to plague her mind about who, what, where, how, and why someone would do this. The answers usually ended up back at working as a paralegal with Skooly's firm and seeing that worker's compensation case.

She reached into her purse for the cell phone, removed its radiation protection cover and installed the battery and called him.

He answered on the fourth ring.

7.

Richie Granger first worked as an attorney in Va. Beach, Virginia with Mellis, Wofford, and Bishop as a general practitioner feeling his way around the legal community and looking for a niche to excel.

But he found himself in the middle of a good old boy network -- where lawyers knew the judges and the judges knew the lawyers, and the judges received their judicial appointments through legislative lawyer buddies which would get favorable court client rulings. In general, the outcome of any proceeding would favor the good old boy network unless an antagonist like Richie kept his litigations in the Circuit Court and threatened a jury trial at each pre-trial hearing.

"You know, a lot of people don't like you," one of the old timers said. "You tie up the dockets with unnecessary actions and think it's a grand old world where everything goes right."

It does when the law is on my side, Richie thought, *and if you haven't paid off that particular judge.*

Richie let the remark slide.

Now at 32 years old, he was a little wiser and just as bold, just in a different community and working product liability cases. And there were a lot of them: airbags in vehicles malfunctioning, inferior construction materials, and contaminated pet foods topped the list.

He loved it, because he was holding large companies accountable for their actions after they had been cheating the public with inferior products.

At 6' and 181 pounds with black hair that was combed straight back and a medium-sized frame, he was not a muscle man but walked humbly in the community and usually with a notebook cradled under his arm with the latest copy of the Virginian-Pilot newspaper, which boasted some of the best writers and news in America. Everything from the latest sports box scores, port activity of foreign ships arriving and departing, military news, and building activity was right there. Occasionally George Fridell would have a mom and pop story of old Tidewater.

Richie had just reached across his desk to pick up a legal file when his phone beeped: it was Marcia calling his private number.

He answered and said, "Hi."

"They're burning me up! I was sitting at my computer and felt a burning sensation on my head!"

Richie was aware somewhat of Marcia's situation but sometimes wondered if she just wasn't imagining things. But then again, he knew what evil people could do, after being in Va. Beach for years.

"Who's burning you up?" he responded.

"The people that work for Skooly. I know it's him. This has been going on ever since I saw that worker's compensation case about using energy on a poor soul and making money off him with the insurance division of the State. I had to leave the apartment."

"Where are you?"

"On Interstate 64 West."

"And just where might you be going?"

"I don't know. I could go to mom's house in Fairfax but I need to stay around here to answer my job applications. I'm scared to go back home. You know someone has been entering my apartment and drugging my foods and messing with my clothes."

"Okay. Okay, Go over to the condo and relax. I have a conference here at 4:30 and will be home at 6:00; then we can talk about it."

"Thank you so much! I'll repay you anyway I can."

"Promise?"

"Cross my heart and love is the answer."

"That's a deal."

Marcia stopped off at Fresh Market's Food store and got some bags of mixed salad greens, steaks, baking potatoes, and a bottle of wine. She paid for the groceries, walked out to the parking lot and began to relax thinking of better times.

But two rows across from her Honda sat a man who stared at her from a late model black Audi.

She smiled to see if that got his attention, and when it did, she figured the stranger was one of her stalkers.

Before she could get the car's license number or get a picture, he quickly backed up and left the parking lot.

She thought about the situation but there was nothing she could do about it right now: she wasn't about to let these stalkers dictate her movements and life. Besides, it was Thursday night and she wanted to enjoy the upcoming weekend.

She got back on Interstate 64 and exited onto Parkway Road. She admired the plantation farms on the way to Williamsburg. The scenery here was always pretty because there weren't any buildings for miles and the crepe myrtle trees hung along the sides of the roads glistening with shiny bark coverings. Pebbled roads, white fences, and long driveway entrances to private homes with iron fencing surrounded gardens and parks.

Marcia thought back to Colonial America and the people who lived here: tobacco farmers, fishermen, blacksmiths, traders, and a host of politicians who frequented the governor's mansion and Raleigh's Tavern at Williamsburg.

And then there was nearby Jamestown, the first town settlement in America in 1609 with a small group of people who lived in just a few buildings.

Many of the people died that first winter in America of cold, starvation, or attacks by the Indians. Nearby, in the river at Yorktown, are replicas of boats that had brought

144 people to Jamestown: the Godspeed, Discovery, and the Susan Constant.

Marcia left the parkway and turned onto Cobblestone Road and stopped at a gate where a uniformed guard recognized her.

He gave her a nod of approval, and after the gate was opened, she drove into the community.

She admired the fountains of water and the summer lilies surrounding the middle fountain area and pulled into an empty spot next to Richie's car, a red Toyota Camry. She got out of the car and walked to his 2nd-story condo. It was 6:00, and he was home.

She knocked on the door.

"Come in and I'll be out in a minute," Richie yelled.

"Okay." And she quietly walked into the living room wondering if she should even be here. She knew what would probably happen, but what was she supposed to do? Seeing his school boy frame, smelling the Old Spice fragrance, and hearing his confident sweet words always made her feel safe and peaceful, among other things, like sensuous.

"Got the dinner goods," she yelled.

She put them on the tiled kitchen counter and dropped her purse on the couch along with her aching back.

She sat and thought while looking at the colonial pictures on the wall of patriots marching, women sewing quilts, and men making corn meal from turning stones of a horse drawn wheel.

Richie entered dressed in a teal green golf shirt, gray cotton sweat pants and looking exclusively handsome with dark hairy arms and a tanned face.

Now she knew why she was here.

But her fears were real and she began talking about them. "I was so close to finding the location of their targeting system and computer server address when I started getting hurt."

Richie nodded slightly while looking at the T-bone steak, salad packs, green peppers, onions and a baked potato that lay on the counter. He was hungry.

Marcia was still nervous, so she went to the counter and opened the wine bottle. She poured some in a frozen glass she got from the freezer. She took a big swallow and finally calmed down.

He looked at her stoically wondering about her.

She knew how selfish she was acting, and she went to him.

"I'm sorry." She bowed her head and laid it against his chest.

But she couldn't yet quit talking about what happened. "The coordinates showed a spot near Australia, and then I started getting hurt," she said as she meekly looked up at him.

"Well, that narrows it down," Richie said, as he turned aside from her.

Marcia held her glass away and looked away lost in her train of thought:

"Well, they're also not that far away with the idiot nearby who keeps coming into my apartment. It's

29

obviously synchronized somehow and coordinated by someone who knows what I'm doing every minute of the day."

He calmed her again by patting her on the back and hugging her softly.

"Ummmm . . . Well, at least you made it here and you're safe, and who knows, you may be onto something."

He let loose of her, went and opened the packaged salad greens and put the contents in two bowls. "Maybe you ought to hire a private investigator."

"And just how would I pay for that?"

She went and sat on the couch and thought. "Hey. That's a great idea! I'll be a private investigator."

Richie put two bowls of greens on the dining room table and stared out the window at the maple tree leaves blowing in the wind now at sunset and wondered what he'd just started.

"I'll be a private investigator and find out who is bothering me," Marcia said,

"But you have to get a license."

"No problem. Remember Rufus Stronger at the Hendricks' hearing and how Mr. Hendricks deposed him to tell about Mrs. Hendricks going out and laying in bed with her hairdresser?"

"I could use a private investigator," Richie responded.

"Would after dinner hour be too late?" Marcia said.

"What do you have in mind?"

"An investigating practice," Marcia said as she sipped the last of her wine and finally felt like eating some food now that she had a new direction and some new hope.

"Wouldn't cost much, would it?" Richie asked as Marcia moved closer to him.

"Not for the first hour," she answered as she smiled and moved closer to him and rubbed his head and shoulders.

Richie smiled.

8.

The sun was setting and shadows were creeping along the sidewalk with lights from street lamps flickering on and off just outside of Julian's apartment.

Julian rehearsed the things he had to do to get in Marcia's apartment and make sure no one saw him: wear some dark clothing, make sure the neighbors were not around, quietly open the two locks on the door.

Once entered, he would unscrew the kitchen overhead light slightly to pulse the electricity, disturb her clothing by making a mark on one of her white blouses, and replace the vitamins she kept in the cabinet with a couple of barbiturates. He knew the barbs would knock her out, and if someone was going to implant her, she would be asleep for that time.

He would also use his lighter to heat up a sealed plastic bottle top of a soft drink to loosen the top without breaking the seal and open the top to insert hallucinatory pills. Then he'd screw the top back on – before it cooled.

That should keep her down for awhile or up, he thought.

And then he'd put the bottle back in the lower cabinet where it came from.

He'd unlock a window just to make her worry a little when she found it.

He would take a couple pieces of underclothing and replace some that he had taken earlier, and he would exit the apartment and leave the front door just as he found it.

He was normally used to stealing goods but this was a different program all together -- drugging people's foods and staining clothing.

If Skooly found out Julian had stolen something contrary to the manifest he was given, he could get in a lot of trouble, because overseers of this operation needed to know just what he was doing so they could coordinate electronic actions on the victim and the belongings. Unforeseen actions were a no-no, and for all accounts, he knew the organization was watching him somehow, and they had a lot of power.

Marcia's apartment was a one story ground unit at the end of a complex. When the sun set, Julian easily slipped through a tree lined dark perimeter to find the doorway.

Fortunately, there were no dogs allowed at this apartment complex.

He finished the job and hesitantly looked out the window in the living room to see if anyone was outside. Seeing no one, he left by the front door and locked it from the outside. He replaced the one marker that he had seen.

After this job, he would take some time off, knowing she would probably be scared and stay with her boyfriend.

He might get a call in three weeks to take some of her clothes back -- replace some of what he had borrowed (as Skooly would say), maybe leave the battery caps open on her car battery, or whatever. These actions were designed to bother her confidence and make her forget what she saw on those files at Skooly's office.

Back in the Bougainville bunker, Tori was monitoring the actions of both Julian and Marcia on split screens on a computer monitor.

"She's at her boyfriend's condo and Skooly's ground man went into her apartment and did his job," Tori said out loud to Brahaim.

"Great. Everything's alright then," Brahaim responded. "What about the boyfriend?"

"Boss says he's scared. Already been targeted in the big Tidewater area and run out. He shouldn't be a problem."

"Any lawyer with political connections can be a problem. Worse, if he has principles," Brahaim said.

9.

Rufus Stronger was anything but what his name implied. He was a skinny man with bushy brown hair who grew up in the small community of Chuckatuck just across the peninsula from the James River.

After high school, he had followed the footsteps of his father and harvested clams for a living, until the James River closed to shell fishing because of Allied Chemical's kepone poisoning. It would take years for the river to recover and be open to shell fishing.

So Rufus went to work at the shipyard in Newport News where he interned as a welder.

But he was assigned menial jobs like scraping paint off ships and cleaning below deck storage bins where there was sludge from oil and chemicals.

When he kept being ignored to train for the work he asked for, he decided to investigate the selection process and found unqualified employees were getting the better jobs.

Length of service and best qualified factors were being ignored for advancement. Sifting through paperwork after filing an Equal Employment Opportunity complaint left him disgruntled at the promotion process and looking for another job; hence, Stronger Investigations.

He got sponsored by a local security firm, Shell's Surveillance, for two years.

Now he was on his own: he befriended lawyers, insurance companies, and politicians to provide investigative services throughout the area.

The pay was more lucrative than fishing, especially when the clam harvest declined after the river poisoning. And this job was certainly better than having a boss at the shipyard, who was making him use a time clock for beginning and ending a work shift.

Now he owned a black Honda minivan and basic surveillance equipment. A video recorder, binoculars, a digital camera with a zoom lens along with night vision apparatus, and a computer tablet were all available in the van. Dark clothing hung on hooks. Make-up disguises and several pairs of quiet shoes sat on a side panel shelf.

He rented an office above Ward's Furniture Store, with a view of Main St. in downtown Newport News. It was perfect, and in five minutes, he could get on I-64 and be in Williamsburg within an hour.

The money was good here, from defense contracts at the shipyards and military establishments. Fort Eustis and Monroe were just around the corner.

Rufus was sitting in the front seat of his van on a side street near the intersection of 13th Ave. and Waters Street looking at the back door of a business leased by real estate tycoon Andy Whitten of Hampton.

There was more than a lease violation going on here, Andy had said, with shady late night pickups and early morning off loading actions taking place.

Where were the goods coming from and what were they? Andy wanted to know.

Andy said he had seen some boxes in the warehouse open during an inspection of the fire alarm system.

There were Barbie Dolls, Monopoly Board games, and Sesame Street puppets from a company in Singapore. Neither box nor crate had any stamp of approval or import tag on it.

The goods appeared to be patented goods but made by unlicensed manufacturers, from foreign shell companies making brand names and selling their products in discount stores: they were counterfeit goods. The goods violated patented trademark laws. What caught Andy's attention were boxes of lighter colors and different font script titles from the brands he knew as a youngster.

Stocking goods that were not registered with the Federal Trade Commission or channeled through the Port Authority were illegal.

Rufus didn't know what to think, but if the man was willing to pay him good money for a few hours of surveillance several days a week, then so what.

While Rufus observed, he thought about a message left on his cell phone from a woman named Marcia who offered to be his accomplice. He could use a person like her as a woman -- to distract suspects and to get evidence. And now that he thought about it, she sounded like Marcia Lemay, the transcriber at deposition hearings he had attended to testify about secret events.

It took him a minute to connect the name, but the Hendrick's case was one not likely to be forgotten because Mrs. Hendricks went to a different motel every Friday night to see different lovers. Then he remembered the pretty stenographer at the end of the table adjacent to Mr. and Mrs. Hendricks,

I'd sure like to survey her, he thought pleasantly.

Rufus sat back and put a half-eaten ham sandwich down on the passenger seat. He took out his camera and began to take pictures of the paneled truck that had arrived at the back door of the building. For one thing, the picture was evidence he was doing his job, and for another, this was much better than swinging on a platform peeling and sand blasting paint off ships with air guns on hot humid days over the muddy waters of the Elizabeth River.

But Rufus sure missed those ship laden clams he was using for fishing bait.

10.

Friday morning.

Marcia woke up suddenly and wondered where she was at. Sunlight was pouring in from the kitchen window onto the couch where she had fallen asleep.

Richie's. I'm at Richie's; I came over here after getting burnt at the apartment and talked about something. Oh yes, the investigator job.

She moved slowly across the couch aware of the trauma that came from being under radiological surveillance, but at least she was alive and in one piece, she thought, as she looked down at her body still wondering what had happened and why.

She got up from the couch and saw a note from Richie saying he had gone to work and they'd investigate some other time. He asked her to lock up when she left.

She must have fallen asleep after the wine, but she had an excuse with all the craziness happening around her.

Scared and full of questions about why, who, and how someone was stalking and targeting her remotely, she wanted answers, along with her perpetrators' necks.

And she still needed a job.

She thought about Stronger and opened her purse to find his telephone number on the business card she'd used yesterday to call him. She put the card on the table and picked up her phone and punched in the numbers again.

"Stronger here," he answered, while continuing to look at the back door of the leased building in the early morning before going home and sleeping.

"Hi Rufus, This is Marcia Lemay. Did you get my message last night by any chance?"

"Did. Took me a minute to remember who you are. Why do you want to get in this type of work?" He asked.

The question took Marcia by surprise because she didn't have an answer ready – other than wanting to find her stalkers.

"Well, I need a job for one thing. But I want to catch crooks, people who are cheating on their mates, or just anyone violating the law and costing us taxpayers money," she said trying to cover everything of an investigator's work.

"Fair enough. I could use someone else, and I have a job for you but it's not a high echelon one, but one to get your feet wet and see if you like this type of work."

"Great! A job!" she uttered.

"You got any references?" he asked.

"Uh, yes. I'll put them on a resume sheet and bring it to you."

Stronger noticed the exasperation in her voice and asked why she had quit her job.

Marcia told him about the contract with Skooly and how she came across activity that was less than ethical and wanted no part of it.

"Okay. Come by the office Monday, 2nd floor over Ward's Furniture Store. Mr. Whitten of Bays Real Estate leases a warehouse near the water and wants someone there from 2:00-10:00 p.m. Monday-Friday.

"Well, that sounds okay," Marcia, responded.

"All you have to do is walk along the fenced border every two hours and look for anything that may seem out of line. Journalize your actions. If a vehicle pulls up to the gate, check the manifest for the driver's name, identification number of the truck, and verify the driver's identification. New manifests are issued every month from what I'm told."

Marcia really needed a job and she was almost afraid to ask a question, but she didn't want to jump from hot water into a fire.

"Is this a legal operation?" she asked.

"Far as I know. I don't ask a lot of questions when a client pays me good money to watch a gate and the fenced in area of a warehouse. A truck delivers some kind of goods and the workers repackage them and distribute them to other cities."

"That sounds okay. Sure, I'll take it."

41

"Meanwhile, I'll give you a book to study in preparation for a private investigator's license – to see if you really want to get into this business."

"Well, that's even better. When can I start the job?"

"I'll talk to Whitten but figure on starting Monday at 2:00. First, stop by the office and let's get acquainted. There's a lot of work available we can talk about and I need to show you a few things. Be there at 12:00 Monday."

Stronger is a little bossy but he's also genuine and right now he has work available, Marcia was thinking.

"Okay. See you then. Hey! What should I wear?" she asked.

"Clothes!" Stronger replied.

"I think I understand," Marcia said, and she terminated the call. She smiled a little and thought about her new career as an investigator.

But she had no idea just how much power someone had over her affairs.

Maybe that person wanted her in the job.

11.

The three men in the Bougainville bunker breathed a sigh of relief.

"Okay, we've got her where we want her but she's got closer than anyone to figuring out where we are," the Premiere said. "She must have had tracking software on her computer that escaped our anti-tracking programs and gave location information. But with her being stationary at the warehouse compound during the week, it will be easy to manipulate her locally to get our goods in and out of the warehouse with our drivers. It's the same process we've done to other victims: tire her out nights before shipments arrive from the boat and trucks and keep pressure on her at home. Use modulated wording to her head when needed to make her think she has a wonderful new career. Holograms will still be used on the water to show her things that are not there. She's bound to go crazy at some time."

"What about the boyfriend?" Brahaim asked.

Tori looked away because he really didn't want to hear this conversation but he was committed to the organization and there was no way out until his time was up. Usually that time meant a statute of limitations that had passed for prosecution, which could be years

And even then, he would have to go to a place where he was no threat to the organization -- most likely stuck far away from civilization on a remote island.

"Let him go for now. He's got doubts about her anyway," the Premiere said as he walked away from the console to check on other matters.

Tori was left alone staring at the emotional state of a woman on a computer screen.

Marcia put the phone in her bag and shook herself free of the lint that had gathered on her blouse. She put her tennis shoes on and went to the kitchen for some water and took a long drink. She felt refreshed, but there was work to do. For one thing, she had to get back to her apartment and clean up.

But should she get back on her computer?

She'd think about that when she got there. She turned and looked out the kitchen window to see a clear day. She put the glass down, turned, and grabbed her purse off the coffee table and went and opened the front door and pulled it shut and locked it with a key Richie had given her.

She walked down the one flight of stairs to her car and saw no one looking at her from adjacent homes or nearby cars. She felt calmer, but some odd energy was still hitting her forehead. She could not tell its direction. It could be coming from anywhere with thousands of satellites in space.

She opened the door of her car and got in. Once seated, she reached in the middle console to get her cell phone charger, but it was not there.

She knew had put it there the previous day, but it was gone. She looked on the seat, the floor, the back seat, but it was gone.

And she bowed her head in frustration.

.

12.

Richie got to his workplace an hour late because of an accident that had happened at Patriot Drive and James Road, and there were no alternative routes. A tow truck would be needed to clear the scene.

Richie, always the opportunist, wondered if anyone had gotten hurt and needed legal representation. Vehicle fatalities were a boon to many lawyers, charging insurance companies outrageous fees and claims for injuries. Of course he would be interested in whether a product failed or not.

But sad were firms like Skooly's, whom Richie knew not only had accident hunters for victim representation but staged accident gurus – purposely making accidents and faking injuries.

It took years but insurance fraud investigators finally caught onto the staged accident schemes where the same vehicle – that had been banged up from previous accidents – continued to get in more accidents. Vehicle Identification Numbers and license plates had been changed.

No doubt Skooly and company somehow fixed the ticket violations too.

Richie took a detour and finally got to the office and apologized to Margaret his secretary about being late.

Margaret updated him on the morning's agenda.

She was priceless, knowing most of the judges. She now had twenty years of experience in the legal profession and she kept immaculate records. More importantly, she knew case law about product liability.

"A Mrs. Debreu called this morning," Margaret said as Richie entered the door and starting looking in a pending file on the desk for any awaiting orders or motions for filing at the Clerk of the Court's office.

Margaret sat and looked at the docket of the Circuit Court's civil proceeding on a computer and made sure Richie had not missed any scheduling.

Opposing attorneys were often quick to request and get scheduled hearings without giving notice to all the parties involved.

"And . . . ?" Richie asked.

"Said she'd heard you were a products liability attorney."

"Okay."

"Said her milk tasted funny and wanted to know if you could do something about it."

"Sure. Add some Karo-syrup to make it sweeter."

"Rub by a magnolia bush on the way in?" Margaret asked, since he wanted to be so smart.

Richie always admired Margaret's comments to break the monotony of business.

Richie didn't flinch but wondered if Marcia had left rose fragrance on his collar, which couldn't be a bad thing.

Margaret said, "I know. I know. I hope you wouldn't mind but I told her to call the police and get them to take the carton to the detective's office to get it off to the state laboratory for testing."

"Perfect. What else?"

Judge Farrow called and asked to reschedule the hearing for motions in the Braxtor case until Wednesday the 23rd." He said opposing counsel has agreed."

Richie thought about it a minute and saw no objection to the judge's request; judges don't reschedule arguments unless it's important.

"That's good."

"And that's it for now."

"Okay, I'll be visiting the young man in the hospital who fell off the bicycle because the frame broke."

"And what time should I expect you back?"

"After lunch."

"Sounds good. You want the tape recorder?" Margaret asked.

"Good thinking. Sure. Put it on the desk."

Margaret nodded her head and went to the closet to get it.

Richie went into his office all the time wondering about Marcia and whether he should separate himself from her. He did not need any distractions at this time in life trying to keep his business operating.

He sat down and looked at the painting of a golf course on the wall in front of his desk -- the peaceful grounds of the Bell View Country Club in northern Georgia with its winding creeks and hills that hosted 18 holes of golf with a majestic view of granite rock and a placid lake. It was located far away from Williamsburg but the picture inspired him to look forward to the day when he would retire and play golf three times a week in a cooler climate.

And then he thought about her again: she was smart and pretty; but now like a runaway needing a place to stay because of fear and paranoia.

Or was it? He owed her compassion. If a person loses compassion for the destitute, what purpose would life be? And what if something terrible happened to him, like when he got blackballed in Va. Beach and ran out of town.

There were times in his youth he felt isolation and rejection. The world came down on him, and there was no one to help. If someone did help, they would try and take advantage of his meekness.

"Get rid of him," they would say, as the big boys in the neighborhood would steal his candy and push and rail against him for being skinny and a coward.

He would give Marcia some more time. Things might work out, and he really could use a woman investigator to find a production supervisor's address, specification plans for products, or financial records that seemed to come up missing when trying to figure out the financial worth of a company, and how much they should be assessed liability damages and penalties for making substandard products.

"How much does your company make yearly, Mr. Olteen?" he once asked an accounting manager in a product liability case.

"Well, I'm not sure," he answered.

Richie was flabbergasted, and then he had to ask a whole bunch of questions to finally get the right answer and request copies of yearly income statements.

Company managers often acquire amnesia when questioned about profits when one of their products fails a quality control test and they have to pay victims percentages of gross profits.

Richie rose from his chair and gave the golf course picture one last look. He walked through the door, grabbed the recorder and told Margaret he'd be back after lunch.

He drove to Poquoson General Hospital to see Fredrico, the young man who had suffered a concussion when a bicycle fork tine broke rounding a corner.

While on the way, he thought about his impending argument if the case went to court.

Inferior steel. The Chinese are good at it. They had been mixing cheaper alloys for years – especially plumbing parts.

50

And on this bike, instead of installing lugs for the bicycle frame tubes, the bar tubes were welded to each other.

Instead of solid brake cable wiring, it was stranded. And now there was little room on the axles and handlebars to attach a front basket or rear pannier rack. What was the world coming to when a boy couldn't trust his main mode of transportation?

13.

It was Friday morning and Marcia was on her way home.

She thought about her new job as she drove. She'd be outdoors, mixing with the public and working a night shift which gave her mornings to sun bathe, dry flowers, and get busy studying for an investigator's license.

It all sounded good but life's events never turned out the way she planned, and she didn't understand it. Something was going on and she didn't know why.

She drove into her parking spot and got out.

She looked around the parking area for anything unusual: like vans parked with shaded windshields or long antennas on the roofs, anyone who may be sitting in a vehicle staring, or someone who may be loitering.

She walked on the sidewalk to her apartment and thought about the razor blades underneath the door knob. She approached the door and bent down to see they were still there, but one of the markers in the jamb was gone.

She looked on the threshold and saw it in the corner near the jamb. And this time, she claimed victory.

Now she knew someone had entered the apartment. The marker had been put in there secure, and the rental manager had not notified Marcia of any work to do in the apartment or inspection.

She slowly removed the blades and looked around the area to see if anyone was watching. She smelled the door area for any foreign scents and she wiped the knob with her hand to see if there was any strange residue on it. She opened the door slowly and peeked in. She had every reason to be paranoid after the events of the week.

Nothing was visibly moved.

She dropped her bag on the couch and entered the bedroom and looked at her computer. Everything looked the same, and there was no burning sensation here now.

She relaxed some, thought about vacuuming the rug and cleaning the oven.

Maybe later she'd visit a uniform store and look at buying some dark clothes to look like a guard.

She removed the ribbons from her hair and took off her blouse, pants, shoes, socks, and underwear. She looked at herself in the mirror for a few seconds with sadness about not making love to Richie the previous night but she must have had too much on her mind, and the wine made her tired.

There will be other times, she thought, now that she had a job and felt somewhat alive.

She entered the shower stall and washed away the past couple of days to begin a new day. Finished washing, she reached for a towel – only to find a hole in it and burnt spot in its corner.

And then it started all over again, worrying, imagining someone had come into her bathroom and was out to try and drive her crazy.

"She doesn't know what she's talking about", they would say if she testified against Skooly. "She's crazy."

She felt deflated and worthless.

But she knew truth and facts, and she would not be deterred from the actions of blackmailed perpetrators to suppress her knowledge and God given right to live and prosper.

She could not talk to Richie about this; he already thought she was playing with a loose deck of cards.

But she did have friends in the legal community that had experienced similar incidents.

And the fact was, a marker in the door was on the floor, so someone had been in the apartment. Now she'd be even more determined to find out whom, what, and why.

She called a former court reporter friend, Naomi, who had complained about being stalked and terrorized by a man Naomi had never seen before. The whole affair had driven Naomi to take drugs and make more mistakes at work than ever.

Marcia dried off with the same damaged towel and put on a light blue terry cloth bathrobe and went to the living room to get the phone and punched in Naomi's number.

On the fourth ring Naomi answered and gave a somber hello.

"Oh Naomi. What's going on? This is Marcia."

"Oh, God dear. How are you? I've been thinking about you ever since getting shunned at work."

"Someone is stalking me like you. And now I know what harmful illegal surveillance is because I was sitting at my computer the other day and something started burning me."

"That's what they do when a person is about to expose them. Are you okay?"

"I went over Richie's place and stayed last night."

"Lucky you. With a good man at that. Hopefully he understands the problem."

"I wouldn't go that far with it but I know now what you were going through and I want to end this thing. You think Skooly is involved?"

"Skooly and his cronies are a criminal enterprise that no one seems to be able to stop," Naomi said. "They are certainly involved."

Naomi had recorded court testimony of nearly every law firm in the Poquoson area for twenty years. She knew them all, and that's why she was getting targeted, because she knew about legal cases settled out of court against clients' wishes with judges' permission and signatures behind closed doors.

"They own the judges. Forget reporting to the Judicial Inquiry Commission and the State Bureau of Investigation and even God," Naomi continued.

"Well, there's got to be something that can be done to stop this high tech surveillance of innocent people," Marcia responded.

"Yeah, drop a bomb on their hideout. Now you just go to work and get sweet with that honey of yours and live a happy life."

"I quit my job Naomi."

"Well. Why on earth? Why?"

"I saw some of Skooly's evil works, and since then, I've been stalked like you. I tried to find out who was harassing me via the computer, but my shoulders began burning sitting there. I got scared and grabbed my things and left."

"Oh, dear. Welcome to my world. What are you going to do?

"Well, I think I've got another job with that investigator guy named Stronger. Start Monday at 2:00 on guard duty at a warehouse."

""Stronger is okay, and that sounds like fun. Better than sitting in court all day punching keys.'

"Pray for me Naomi. I plan on getting to the bottom of this and putting these people away."

"Well, good luck honey. Call me when you need some bail money. I'll help out anyway possible. I'm just joking but they do have some connections."

"Yea, yea, I know. Can we get together sometime next week?"

"Just give me a night's notice."

"Okay, it's a deal! Talk later girl," Marcia said, and she tapped the phone's red button to end the call.

Marcia got up from the couch and hung the towel on a line over the washing machine to dry. She looked out the kitchen window to see an overcast day with rain threatening and knew it was an inside day. She thought about Richie and possibly getting together in the evening.

She put on casual clothes and went into the kitchen to get some tea, heat up some water, and put her tea bag in a cup along with some honey.

She got a bagel and sat -- thinking about the evening and her life, and then she began to get very sleepy.

She knew again something was wrong, and she quickly went to the kitchen sink and dumped the tea.

Victory again, she thought.

She boiled some more water and grabbed another tea bag inspecting it, found a packaged sweetener in a cabinet, and opened it and stirred it in her cup of tea.

She was finally winning.

14.

Signal Intelligence Specialist Wilson Wallace was sitting in a bunker at Kunai, Hawaii looking at a computer monitor with a graphic illustration of a spectrum analyzer and scanner that was receiving real time information of electro-magnetic frequency emanations from Papua, New Guinea by order of his commander, Joseph Wainwright.

It wasn't difficult to find transmissions, just to figure out which ones were being used to communicate with a chalet in Switzerland and the United States.

After repeated requests by members of the House of Representative's Armed Services committee and the Department of Defense, something had to be done about the electro-magnetic targeting of the United States that interfered with communications and neurological functions of its people. The Department of Energy had concluded conducting testing non-ionizing radiation fields in the nation and found there was nothing harmful to the population.

But it was coming from somewhere, so the authorities started monitoring terrorist groups such as Zenithe, which had recently been reported to be based in Switzerland and had its tentacles throughout the states.

The trajectory line on the monitor showed brief telephone transmissions to the U.S. and constant computer frequencies emanating from Bougainville, an island north of Australia.

The commander looked over his shoulder and saw it.

"Bougainville. What the hell's in Bougainville?"

"Not much but old mine shafts, dirt roads, and a little landing area," Wilson said. "It used to be an island the Japanese were fighting for in W.W. II, and there's been a civil war there ever since. New Zealand forces occupied it for awhile, and then Australian forces came in and cleaned it up."

"But would there be buildings and communication towers there?" the commander asked.

"Caves are in the hills from mineral exploration," Wallace responded. "Maybe there are hidden antennas in the trees or grounds," Wallace said to Joseph. "But I think that's about as close as we're going to get it with all the humidity in the air."

"Okay. Let the ground guys take over from here. You get any land coordinates for those transmissions? I'll contact those damn civilians in D.C. and give them some of the information. The reverend gets the rest."

"The latitude is 6° South and longitude 155° East."

"That's good enough. Never give those boys the whole story. They think they're so smart to figure out anything anyway. Let them figure out the minutes," the commander finished.

Wallace made the call to F.B.I. headquarters and spoke with one Morgan Stocholm, liaison with the International Police in Australia, New Zealand, and islands of the South Pacific.

Wallace relayed location information for the suspected terrorist group Zenithe at Bougainville, and Morgan said he would handle the case from here and to delete any information acquired for security's sake.

But Morgan knew this case had international consequences and the C.I.A. had jurisdiction over the matter.

He had no idea the C.I.A. was way ahead of him in conducting an operation on the island, but non-communication between intelligence agencies for the sake of bragging rights was usually normal. Neither agency was looking for precious metals on the island – just a control center with computers, antennas, and weaponry.

Randall Levy and Cal Sherwin from the agency had been on the island for three days. They had come as tourists -- hiding their identities of demolition experts and looking to find a storeroom of active computers and antennas that were eavesdropping on communications in America which were attempting to control people via a network of cell phone towers, electrical grid transformers, and microwave dishes.

They sat on the edge of a cotton filled mattress in a dark room where the only light was a ray of sun through the cracks of a wooden door and shuttered window.

"This is not going to work," Randall said as he looked down at a lone rug on an unfinished cement floor. "They know we're here, been watching us like hawks since we got off the boat," he said to Cal.

Cal nodded once in agreement and said, "They got the island surrounded with guards and word has gotten around to the locals. They must be feeding the people with money and food to not talk about the operation. Everywhere we've been; the pleasure cruise boat, rickshaw, town cafes, have all had someone nearby."

"Shall we exit the dreaded place?" Randall asked.

"Could. Might make one and light a fuse before we leave."

"Washington would love that," Randall said. "But how do we get close enough and just where exactly?"

"Got a split fuse to fire both sides of a hill if we have to?"

Randall asked. "Got one to stop the guards from gunning us down as we board a boat?"

"No," Cal responded.

Randall said, "Didn't think so. Stuff your pack and let's get out of here."

The two men opened the two window covers to let in some light and gathered their goods from a headboard and a lone chest of drawers.

They exited the stucco building and walked down the dirt road past some women who were selling baskets from a booth area. Some kids played on the side of the road and a few older men were playing a game of some kind with ivory animal and men pieces.

They turned a corner and walked to a dock 1000 yards away where they knew a boat would take them to the mainland at 10:00, if they were lucky.

15.

Saturday.

Marcia again fell asleep and knew it wasn't all because of a little bit of drugged tea. She could feel forces around her cutting off her blood supply to her head and making her drowsy.

She proved this by getting up slowly and walking to another room that was away from the double living room windows. Immediately, color returned to her face along with some energy.

She brushed her hair and glanced at the clock which now said 12:00.

Oh my God! And she looked over at the phone to see the message light blinking. *I've missed his call!*

She walked over to the answering machine and punched the button to retrieve the message while looking around the apartment and wondering what else had been tampered with, and the recorder said, "Hi sleepyhead, going to play golf at 3:00 this afternoon and will talk later. Bye."

Well that's okay, she thought, and she sat back down wondering what to do about the situation. Nothing was going right. Her linens were being folded differently, someone was stalking her, and now her foods were being drugged.

Sometimes she thought about the silent voices Naomi talked about. They were short phrases saying the words: *good, bad, I love you, beautiful.*

She had tried to drown them out but nothing was working except some crumbled up foil nearby.

By accident, she had balled up some and was ready to throw it in the garbage when suddenly everything got real quiet. Then she remembered Naomi saying something about crumbled up foil scattering GPS frequencies.

She was losing her confidence -- but not her faith. Marcia Lemay had grown up in the Bow Creek section of Virginia Beach.

Daughter of Greer and Roberta Lemay, she had two younger brothers she looked after while their dad was sea bound in the Navy six months of every year and her mother was out partying.

It was difficult, keeping her brothers out of the local ditches and fights with the neighborhood kids. And her mother would go out at night with friends and not come home until early in the morning usually slurring words and staggering.

She'd tell Marcia before she left in the evenings, "Just make sure they stay in and I'll see you in the morning."

The officers club down the road was becoming more of a home to Roberta Lemay than the home in Bow Creek. But these things happen when a sailor husband is deployed away from home for extended periods of time.

So Marcia began to look for the right way to live. She started attending a local Episcopalian Church two blocks from home. It was a strange sight at first, looking at its weathered brick exterior walls and walnut front door that looked like an entrance to a mausoleum.

On the lawn was a white wooden cross with Jesus on a marble platform. On the other side of the lawn was a plain wooden cross with a purple robe draped over it.

The side door of the church looked like mahogany, with its red tint and medium grain. The walkway was a perfect bed of shells smoothed off with coarse mortar, like some ivory mottled entrance to a stairway to heaven.

Maybe this church and grounds had been built in colonial times but the beauty of it made it archaically heavenly.

Marcia felt close to God each time she walked towards the church, and finally one Sunday morning, she walked into an empty sanctuary and accepted Jesus as her Savior.

The formality of the worship services did not bother her.

The singing, responsive readings from the Bible, and observing symbolic communion by breaking bread and drinking wine of the body and blood of Christ inspired her to perform God's work in some way. At least she knew what she was doing, and what was happening in the church. At home, she didn't know what was happening one minute from the next.

There was no fighting here at church. There was no arguing or distraction. She felt peace. And she learned there was a higher power here on earth.

As it is in heaven, so shall it be on earth, she would think.

This power was higher than her parents at home, the judge in the courtroom, or a group of lawyers – all who seemed to have prideful dispositions of character fluffed up in the world.

But this divine power came through the blood of Jesus and she acknowledged she wasn't good enough to live by her own standards. She needed help -- and divine forgiveness for her misgivings.

Her father had eventually got land duty and things calmed down around home for awhile, but Marcia planned to make her getaway despite any family reformation. She would learn a job skill, find a job, and have a place to live.

After reading books about unsolved crimes, she decided on being a court recorder after high school -- to get some accountability in the world.

But she didn't figure on being in the middle of a crime scene, with a third party trying to wreck her life.

She wasn't foolish enough to think she could solve this problem on her own, but with God's spirit, she would have victory. And a good man companion could be worth his weight in gold.

She knew she needed one, after seeing how elderly couples at the church interacted and seemed happy as two people could be.

She admired the couples that had been together for decades, enjoyed prosperity, and good health.

And that's what she wanted. She knew her role, and she wanted to know his.

She picked up the phone and called him, and he answered on the third ring.

"Hello," he answered.

"Richie, how are you?"

"Okay. Played a short round of golf after a little work and got to talk with a few friends. And you sleepyhead?"

Marcia subtly bowed her head in shame for a second and didn't quite know what to say. *Was it about the long nap this morning also?* She thought. "I'll make it up to you."

"Sounds good but that's two make-ups."

"Okay! Two make-ups. So where do we start?"

"Brouhards. 6:00. I'll pick you up at 5:45."

"No. I'd rather my car be over there if that is okay," Marcia said.

"That's fine. Be here at 5:30," Richie said.

"What's the dress there? I've never been," Marcia anxiously responded. She felt Richie carrying her into a new world wherever they went and it was so exciting to be with him.

"Come as you are but most people wear something nice. It's a dinner playhouse and semi-formal is the norm."

"That sounds great. There's a play there too?"

"Yes, and I'm sure you'll like it."

"Okay, I trust you. I'll be ready with two make-ups."

"Yeow."

16.

Sitting over a glass of wine at the dinner theatre, Marcia was awed by the scene around her of thirty tables seated with well dressed couples and large pictures of colonial architecture and ocean going vessels on walls in the background.

Another wall showed a Victorian painting of a lady who wore a feathered hat and red petticoat with white ruffles while fanning herself and sitting on a leather chair with brass rivets.

The stage was in front of Richie and Marcia with a purple curtain drawn across its middle.

Marcia imagined actors and stage props in back of the curtain.

Lights directed at the stage reflected off the oak polished floor.

Waiters, who were all men, were dressed in black pants, white shirts, and black bow ties. Their shoes were black and polished. The men walked graciously across the floor taking food and drink orders from the attendees. It was 6: 15 and the show would begin at 7:00.

Marcia shifted in her seat and looked at Richie in his navy blue blazer with a starched collared light yellow cotton shirt. She admired his lean tanned face that came from being outdoors, and she thought *Lord, am I good enough for this or what?*

As if reading her mind, he said, "You look nice tonight."

Marcia blushed somewhat and bowed her head slightly as if to remember what she had on, which was a teal green, orange, and black floral print dress that contrasted nicely with her blond hair. She wore a black pearl bracelet. On a seat beside her sat her purse – a rush weaved bag accentuated with pastel colored cloth on its perimeter.

The bag was one of her favorites, having been made in Thailand with a brown cane handle that was polished to show its dark grain. She may be living in a crowded low income suburban apartment complex but she certainly remembered how to dress.

"Well, thank you Mr. handsome. You look nice yourself," she responded and smiled.

The dinner would come soon, with Marcia having ordered a Caesar's salad and plate of fresh baked flounder in a sour cream sauce. On the side would be a baked potato with shredded cheddar cheese and broccoli, and a coleslaw dish with fresh grated carrots.

Richie went for fried oysters, black rice, and asparagus with a cream sauce.

When the food arrived, Marcia bowed her head and said a little blessing. She didn't know if Richie was ready to hear her prayers publicly but it wouldn't stop her from personally praying to a god she knew was real and gave her peace and direction.

The lights dimmed, as if God had just closed his eyes, and Marcia felt such a religious connotation at this most unusual time she shed a tear.

The velvet curtains drew back to each side of the stage with a backdrop of a street setting and lone beggar sitting on a chair jiggling a cup.

The play would replicate the story of the good Samaritan in the scriptures with people passing by and looking in the cup, doing a dance, and giving nothing. The old beggar man would be saddened and show it with a repertoire.

And finally, there was a glorious celebration when a kind man came by and gave his only coin from a ragged pocket.

The play was very colorful with bright clothes. And there was a musical score that went along with the actions of each scene.

This is nice, Marcia thought. She didn't have to talk much here with the actors performing; she was still plagued by the events of the past few days.

But she had to go on with life and try to be normal, go out and have some fun. And Richie was part of it. Surely he would understand.

When the play was over, drinks were still being served.

"Can we stay a little longer?" Marcia asked.

"I think we have a half hour or something like that. The waiters will begin to pick up dishes though."

"That play was very nice, and I'm glad the poor man finally got some cash to buy some food."

Richie nodded.

"So how was your visit with Fredrico?" Marcia asked.

"He's becoming more aware of things. Still a little fuzzy from the fall but talks good."

"So how does one verify a bicycle fork tine was made of inferior steel?" she asked.

"Oh," Richie said, as he was finishing the last of his meal. "The most common way is to send it to a metallurgist who has testing equipment, but then what are the standards for a bicycle fork tine to carry a 65 pound kid going around a corner at 10 m.p.h. on an asphalt road on a 90 degree day and not break?"

"Well, I wouldn't know. But there's bound to be a way to find out."

Richie nodded absent mindedly and said, "And there's a way find out the proprietary ingredients in Kellogg's Cornflakes."

"Okay. I get it. It gets complicated."

"Well, not really. The defense will not reveal the composition of the metals, admit there is a problem which can be fixed, and to save money will make a deal with my client. No problem there. That's money!"

"Oh you lawyers are always one step ahead of everyone."

"But not you."

"No. Not me, I have the rest of the evening planned out."

"Will there be any deals?"

"You bet. Let's go."

17.

Richie wiped his mouth with his napkin and put some money on top of the waiter's bill in a tray and got up from his seat to escort Marcia to the car. He was proud to do it. Marcia had had excellent manners and was a good conversationalist, especially when he needed feedback on important matters.

When in the car, Richie asked, "So what do you think happened to each of the people who did not put any money in the beggar's cup?"

"Well, there's an old proverb about the liberal being made fat," she replied.

"Fat? What's food got to do with this?" he asked.

"I'm not talking about food. I'm talking about kindness. It means that someone who is liberal with their kindness, time, and assets, will receive something back multiplied. Those who don't give are robbed of a blessing."

"Well, what about those people who don't have anything for the cup?"

"The good Lord understands: one of them gave a smile; the other a dance, and one showed compassion and gave the beggar a hug. Everyone who is familiar with poverty knows there is hurt and pain from being impoverished. And they will show compassion in some way."

Richie could only wonder. He'd actually had it pretty good in life growing up with parents who had good jobs and money.

"That makes sense. It was a wonderfully scripted play and the actors were brilliant." Riche said.

Marcia said nothing but let him think about what he had just said.

With lights from the parkway reflecting off the pebbled road, Richie turned into his parking area with a much better feeling about Marcia than he had earlier in the morning.

"Won't you come in?" he asked.

"Well, yes, and thank you for taking me to Brouhards. It was fantastic."

Entering the living room, Marcia wondered what she could do to make up for her recent selfishness. She saw dirty dishes in the sink, so she put her purse on the dining room table and walked over to the sink to wash them.

But she certainly had another idea; they had been together long enough and they were grown adults.

Richie said nothing as he took off his coat and sat on a stool at the bar counter that divided the living room from the kitchen.

While washing, Marcia turned her head and said, "This is one of my make-ups."

"What's the other one?" he asked.

Marcia pointed her head at the bedroom door, "In there. Go make yourself comfortable and I'll be in shortly."

"Yes ma'am," Richie said with a smile on his face.

Richie admired her take charge attitude at times. His mother certainly never showed it, but she never needed to. His father was the leader in the family and a good one at that. He worked a steady accountant's job, came home after work, and spent free time with the family. Both his father and mother were strict Presbyterians who knew the responsibilities of husband and wife, and they abided as such.

After high school, Richie had attended Old Dominion University in Norfolk and got a degree in Business Administration. It was at Old Dominion he realized he needed to toughen up mentally if he was going to be competitive in the business world, so he joined the fraternal organization of Pi Delta Pi.

He did not have any brothers or sister growing up, so this was a good opportunity to understand people better and interact socially.

After graduation, he saw little opportunity to make good money with a business degree, knowing people or not.

But when his father had an accident when the metal frame of a lawnmower collapsed prematurely from rusted bolts and the cutting blade underneath threw a rock from out underneath and cut his leg, Richie wanted accountability. It wasn't a big accident, but one that would motivate him to attend law school and learn the legal system.

Richie attended law school at the University of Virginia.

Upon graduation and passing the bar exam, he came back to the Tidewater area to work.

Richie had had a close relationship with a girl at UVA but both of them realized it was interfering with their long term goals. She would be moving to Alaska, to work in her major and biologically test cold weather wildlife resistant bacteria.

Richie hadn't even thought of another woman until Marcia came along. Maybe it was time to be with someone, time to become serious, now that he had his business established.

But Lord knows she was so much bolder than him. Where he didn't have confidence, she knew exactly what to do. When he didn't know what to say in public, she easily spoke the words, and when things went wrong, she got back up and went onto something else.

"Things will work out," she'd remark.

And so he lay on the bed thinking about things: the evening, Fredrico, work cases at the office, golf, and Marcia. And he felt good,

The lights dimmed when Marcia came into the room. She went to the other side of the bed near the window and sat down on the edge of the bed.

She changed into a lightweight sheer cotton top from an overnight bag she had been keeping at the condo. And she slid under the covers and snuggled against him.

She looked up at him and said, "Thank you so much Richie for this evening," and moved her right hand to rest on his breast.

"It was nice," he responded.

After a pause, Marcia eased on top of top of him and waited -- and they made love for the longest time in response to each other.

Afterward, Marcia cleaned them up and lay down with her right hand on Richie's left chest and her head down on his right shoulder; they were asleep in minutes. They would wake up in the same position as sunlight slowly streamed over their faces with a warmth unparalleled.

And they caressed each other softly.

"Where did you learn that?" he asked.

She smirked and said, "Yoga class."

She smiled a bit and softly put her finger to his lips and drew it down to seal them and said, "Quiet. It's still early."

18.

Marcia woke up first from their extended stay in bed.

It was 11: 00, Sunday morning and she felt like she should be in church after all those years of depending on God as a teenager.

But here, she had security in Richie – from unknown perpetrators watching and plaguing her. She lay in bed for a few minutes and wondered about it all.

She slipped out from beneath a lone sheet and put her feet on the floor. Her hair was a tangled mess, so she walked to the bathroom and found a brush to straighten it while Richie was still sleeping.

She returned to find her clothes on the night stand where she had left them. She dressed and walked to the living room trying to make sense of the last 24 hours. She sat down on the couch and said a prayer.

Lord, I don't know how all this is going to turn out but I'll try to go about life and enjoy it, and I will glorify you in all that I do.

But the subliminal suggestions were still there; *you're a tramp, and ugly. You can't do that. Go home!*

She knew they were being artificially processed from what Naomi had told her about silent sound technology. Naomi just didn't know where they were coming from, but from the wireless technology that was sweeping the planet.

Down with the towers! Marcia urged in thought. *Someone has got to turn off the energy to those antennas!*

Marcia tried to dismiss the modulated words to her throat and head. She said another prayer against them.

But she got scared again and wanted to stay with Richie forever. Here, she got some relief, and security. Everything was so mixed up.

She got up and went into the kitchen to make some tea. She boiled some water, grabbed two tea bags out of the cabinet, and stirred some honey into a couple of cups. She had heard Richie showering.

And she thought about last night.

The love was certainly relieving, but it couldn't continue in this situation.

She wondered about the day. What was she going to do about the situation?

When he entered the room, he came to her and gave a big hug. He was dressed casually in a bone colored golf shirt and dark blue cotton running pants. He looked content.

When he let go of her, she added two slices to the tea cups.

"You're an amazing woman," he said.

And she answered, "You're an amazing man."

One thing she had learned with men is to complement their complements, but if they went astray, she'd speak her mind of truth.

Richie looked out the window to see a clear day with sunshine. "Be nice to take a little walk later."

"Oh, honey. It sounds good, but I should really be going. I've already extended my stay."

"But not your energy," he responded.

She blushed. "No. Still have that. Want a bagel?" she asked as she slipped off a plastic retainer clip from a bagel bag and wanting to change the subject.

"Sure, then can we walk?"

"Okay, but we could attract attention."

Richie grabbed a bagel from her hand and said, "I hope so."

After they finished the bagels and tea, both headed down the stairs and onto the walk that surrounded the inner perimeter of the condominiums.

They admired the trees with fresh new spring leaves, the squirrels looking for buried nuts and acorns, and the birds scurrying to find nest materials.

"Oh, look. There's a woodpecker on that pine tree," Marcia said.

"Very pretty," Richie answered.

"It's so beautiful here Richie. You have done well for yourself," Marcia said.

"It's been a lot of work to get this far, with all the trouble I went through at Virginia Beach."

"Well, life has its troubles. We are to be faithful to work through them and trust God who is in control. He wants the best for us," Marcia said.

They continued to walk around the perimeter while the sun began to peek through the trees and warm the grounds. Summer would he here soon, and air conditioners would be humming while water from condensate drains would find its way to the ground and across sidewalks.

A fox squirrel stood on its hind legs and looked at them as if begging for food. And there was a fountain of water where ducks gathered at the edge and absorbed the cool mist from the spray pattern.

It was too nice of a weekend to spoil it talking about surveillance. Marcia avoided it completely though she felt a high frequency sound whiz by her ear on a couple of occasions while they were walking.

She dared not mention the drone flying over during the walk. No. Her time would come to get her attackers. This was Sunday, and Richie deserved some time for keeping her. She never should have said earlier that she had to be going. What was she thinking?

They returned to the condo, and she stayed another hour; then she said bye and kissed him.

She really was anxious to get back to her apartment to make sure things were okay.

Tomorrow would be a new day, with a new job.

19.

Marcia got into her car and backed out of the driveway while suspiciously looking in all directions for anyone who may be watching her.

She took off down the road with a glare on the windshield from the sun and headlights of passing cars bothering her vision. She reached for her sunglasses in the console, but they were not there.

She felt all around the console while she was driving, but they were not there. Finally, she slowed the car down and looked in the compartment: they were still not there.

It didn't surprise her. She had had a good time, and one thing the perpetrators do is get jealous of victims that have a good time; so they play little tricks on the victims.

The perpetrators were also letting her know they knew where she was.

Possibly they took the glasses while she was at the dinner theatre, or maybe it was when she was with Richie and slept well, which is also what Naomi had warned about: "If you sleep well, it's because the perps have harassed you for a couple of nights and then on the third night, you are so tired you won't wake up when they are bothering your vehicle or entering your home. Sleep deprivation is part of the program, to have the victims make mistakes, get in accidents, and have bad health.

Marcia swore revenge on these people. When she got home, she called Naomi to share what had happened.

"They stole my sunglasses!" Marcia said to her.

"Be glad they didn't damage your car. I know people who say these idiots take off battery caps, radiator caps, put pine straw on top of the engine to catch fire, and a host of other things."

"My God, who are we dealing with here?"

"Criminals. Straight out of the synagogue of Satan. Your guess is as good as mine but Mr. S. is a good place to start," Naomi said, not wanting to specifically say Skooly, the old attorney. "How's lover boy?"

"Okay, he can be a sportster sometimes but we had a great night last night. Went to Brouhards for a great meal and show."

"I've been there. It's quite a place. Try their scallops in butter and homemade bread sometime."

"The fresh flounder was excellent. Richie had oysters and some black rice which I didn't know existed. I had a taste and it was smoother than regular rice."

"They got everything seafood -- comes off the boat at Point Comfort. I didn't know until last week but that's where the first slaves landed in America. Used to be a restaurant near there called The Sea Traders, but the name was changed because of the history around the Point. Now it's The Sea Galley. They'll have a twelve pound bluefish decked out on a buffet line on weekend nights with all the toppings. But the last time I went there the perps did something to my food, so I stopped going."

"What did they do Naomi?"

"Well, maybe it was the water or something but my throat started swelling up. Maybe they hired the waitress to make me sick. I saw her take a break shortly after I ordered. She went and talked on the phone for a few minutes."

"Oh, Naomi. They don't do that."

"Oh Marcia, they do do that; so beware. These idiots own restaurants, waitresses, and food -- and don't drink any unopened drinks at home!"

"Well, there have been incidences at home where I've been wondering about the food and drinks."

"Be careful darling, call me when you need."

"Okay. Thanks for listening." And Marcia terminated the call.

It was late Sunday afternoon and Marcia laid down for a rest. She was still thinking about what Naomi had said.

After a few minutes of rest, she got up and went to make sure everything was okay in the kitchen. She went through all her cabinets and inspected cans, spices, and dried goods.

She looked for anything out of place. She looked at the cabinet doors for any strange hand prints. She felt something different about the floor in front of the kitchen cabinet: it felt depressed, like someone heavy had recently stepped on it.

She couldn't have done that, she thought. She only weighed 112 lbs.!

She went back to the bedroom somewhat relieved and thinking, *Maybe I'll be a good investigator after all.*

She lay out some gray slacks, a navy blue knit sweater, black socks, and a pair of black leather ankle boots to wear for Monday morning. She also got a compact digital camera out of the closet, a notebook, and a small flashlight and put them all in a separate bag. What more could she need.

Then she went to the 2nd bedroom and her computer to check her e-mail. She turned the computer on and went to her e-mail account. There were trivial advertisements about new food supplements, books for sale, and a response to an apartment inquiry she had made under pressure last week.

She deleted them all and wondered if she should engage her tracking software to see if Mr. Nosy was snooping on her again.

How can one person have so much power to use a remote energy source and hurt people?

She thought about it for awhile, and then decided against searching him out. After all, it was Sunday.

She wanted to concentrate on getting the new job tomorrow, and Richie. He was the bright spot in her life, maybe forever.

The phone interrupted her thinking. *And how is it that every time I start thinking about finding the source of the targeting, some noise or distraction occurs. If it isn't the phone, it's a loud muffler outside, or a plane suddenly descends. Am I just being too paranoid?* She asked herself.

She answered on the fifth ring.

"Hey, you've made it home. How are you?"

It was Richie.

Marcia relieved, said, "Fine, fine, just laying out some clothes for tomorrow." She tried not to sound too anxious.

But he sensed the worry in her voice.

"It will be alright Miss Sherlock Holmes."

"Now you're the confident one."

"We lawyers get like that."

"Is it a natural thing or did you learn that in law school?"

"Comes from experience," Richie answered. "You got experience."

Marcia giggled a little and said, "Yeah, I guess I do, but not always in the right place."

"Was the other night."

"Oh, that." And Marcia changed the subject. "Got a big day tomorrow?"

"Drafting a bill of complaint against Mr. Bicycle Company and getting some medical reports about Fredrico. After lunch, I'll be researching legal cases about chemical spills at military bases and who's responsible for that.

"Sounds interesting, and thank God for Margaret, one of the best."

"She is. What time do you expect to be home tomorrow?"

Marcia, now worried more than ever that someone was listening to her phone conversations told Richie she wasn't sure; she would call him – Tuesday -- and let him know all about the new job.

She wished him a good day at work and ended the call.

She sat gazing out the window at a streetlamp and saw it flicker occasionally, though there was still sunlight on the pole. She wondered what that was all about.

She again figured the perpetrators were using some kind of radar on her since she was able to divert the signal at times with foil – and that it was probably interfering with the sensor on the light – tricking it into thinking the sun was coming up and turning the light off and on.

But what did she know? She was just an ordinary woman needing a job. At 9:00 she went to bed, and finally an hour later, drifted off to sleep with a pillow over her face.

20.

Awakened early in the morning by a pulsing to her nervous system did nothing to allay her fears someone was using high tech energy fields to disturb her, if not disable her. She rolled over on her side periodically trying to get rest but nothing worked.

Twenty minutes later, it was 6:00 a.m. and she could still not figure out where the pulsing was coming from. She could call the apartment manager to make sure the wiring was correct, or maybe there was someone nearby operating a generator.

But she was thankful to see the dawning of another day. *Rejoice in the Lord,* she thought. *And I have a job!*

She had plenty of time to get dressed and get herself in shape to go to work, since she did not have to see Rufus until 12:00. She read a little while, had a cup of safe tea, and watered some of her indoor plants. She also packed some snacks for her stay at the booth.

Ready to go at 11:30, she grabbed her bag and the markers for the door. She locked the door and drove the 15 minutes to Ward's Furniture Store in Newport News.

It was an old brick building that was two stories tall and used to have furniture stocked upstairs – until business slowed and people began buying furniture from large discount retailers.

Ward's furniture turned that 2nd floor into office space. Rufus Stronger found it when he was drinking coffee at Rosie's Café across the street and saw a For Lease sign on the door.

Stronger liked the upstairs office because there was a private entrance, a security system was in place, and there was plenty of lighting with two rows or fluorescent lights on the ceiling.

Better yet, the one window in area had a nice view of downtown. He could look out the window to see the street below and some stores along Main Street in both directions.

He had leased the 400 square foot area for $500 a month with a three year lease agreement.

It was big enough for a writing desk, a couple of bookshelves, a couple of chairs; a desk for his computer, printer, and fax machine. And there was a private parking area in the back of the building along with street parking for visitors out front.

Marcia arrived at 11:45 and parked on the street in front of Ward's.

She put a quarter in the parking meter for a one hour fee. She found the private entrance door in front that was painted with the words *Stronger's Investigative Service*.

She opened the door and walked up creaky wood steps to knock on a six paneled wooden fir door.

"Come in!" yelled Stronger.

His voice sound strong and confident.

Stronger had already seen Marcia park out front and was expecting her.

Marcia entered the door while looking around the room at the same time complimenting him on the décor.

The room had a couple pictures on the walls of shrimp boats and James River watermen sitting on old barrels sewing up damaged nets.

There were ceramic figures of dolphins on Rufus's desk, and an old floor lamp with stained glass was in the corner of the room. The brown commercial carpet, pine ceilings, and beaded wallboard all fit together to make the place cozy.

"Nice place Rufus. But that door there. Is there cement in it or something?"

Rufus smiled a bit and said, "It's made of fir and full of oil put on by the owner of the store. Said it was an original that his granddaddy made a hundred years ago, so he preserves it with oil every fall before winter. An oldie but goodie. Many of the items in here are from the furniture store downstairs. The owners lease me this place. Come in and have a seat and let's get started."

91

Stronger cleared a few things from his desk and looked Marcia in the eye and asked once more why she wanted to do this work.

"Rufus, I'm not going to lie to you. I got someone bothering the hell out of me and I'd like to know a little about this business, plus I need a job."

Rufus thought about it for a second while listening to the traffic outside getting noisier because people were taking lunch breaks.

A sound of a motorcycle raced by. A five ton cargo truck with canvas over its rear bed ground through a couple of gears before getting up some speed. And diesel smoke drifted up towards the office window.

Heat pump compressors were turning on and off as the day was warming and humidity was finding its way on shore from the Chesapeake Bay.

Rufus turned his head back towards Marcia and said, "Not your boyfriend is it?"

"I don't know who it is," Marcia said.

"And what may I ask happened to the job with Skooly's firm?" Rufus said, having already figured out why Marcia was being harassed.

Marcia hesitated a second, being unsure whether to tell Rufus everything, *but my goodness he's an investigator,* she thought.

"Not everything was kosher there Rufus, and I didn't want any part of it."

"Doesn't surprise me. Skooly's been known to work the bad side. Well, you could always stay in the business of transcribing."

"It's time for something different. Are you going to help me or not?" she boldly asked Rufus.

"Okay, okay, just want to see how serious you are. Business gets hectic here at times and there is some pressure to find out who wants to know what or get what ain't there. I get jobs that no one else seems to figure out how to do."

"I'm interested or I wouldn't be here," Marcia responded. "And I want to find the person harassing me. But investigative work is something I've had in the back of my mind for years. I mean, sitting behind a keyboard all day in stuffy lawyer offices hearing people lying about this and that gets old. When testimony doesn't go right for them, I often get blamed. They say I've misinterpreted their words or something."

She didn't want to tell Rufus everything she saw at Skooly's a week ago, so she stopped talking.

"Go on," Rufus said, seeing that Marcia had more on her mind.

"Well, that's basically it," she responded. And she shifted her legs a little and set her purse down.

"Well, now sitting in a car for an hour or more in the middle of winter looking for someone to come out of a house isn't exactly stimulating either." He waited for a response.

"Well, what else do you do?" she wondered.

"Well, I go to the police station on occasion and dig up reports on individuals, submit FOIA requests, talk to newspaper reporters, and follow people around."

93

"Following people around sounds interesting. That's what someone's doing to me," Marcia said.

"And sometimes the hours are late at night and other times very early in the morning," Rufus said.

Marcia needing a job said, "Well that's all fine with me, and I don't mind being a security guard."

"Okay. You start at 2:00 today."

"Wow. That was fast. Don't you want to know anything else about me?"

"Already do. You're the daughter of the Lemays, have two brothers, lived in Va. Beach for seventeen years and went to Key's Business School. You had a boyfriend named Chan, a boy from Thailand who was training here for aircraft maintenance and now you see Mr. Granger on occasion."

"Rufus, isn't that an invasion of my personal life?"

"That's what I do. I invade peoples' lives, but I don't touch. That's for Captain Tellis downtown or whoever has jurisdiction over the area. I want to know who's working for me."

"Okay. How I do I look?"

"Good. Might lay off some of the make-up though. We like to blend in with the crowd and not stand out, unless you're trying to get attention."

"What kind of attention?" Marcia asked.

Rufus smiled a little and said, "Girl attention."

"Feel like a bit to eat before we go?" Rufus asked.

"No. Not really. Well maybe something light. Is there something available at the job site?"

"No," Rufus responded.

"Okay, that's fine. I'll have a sandwich or something."

And Rufus reached in his desk drawer to get a few items and put them on the desk.

"So what are those things?" Marcia asked.

"This contraption here is high powered flashlight, one like the police use."

"I brought a flashlight."

"Not like this one." And Rufus picked it up and shined it at the wall to show the bright light. "The beam will light up anything for a few hundred yards."

"Oh," Marcia said as she humbly put her pen light back in her purse.

Rufus picked up a card with a metal backing and pin attached. "And this is an identification badge that says you are an employee of Stronger's Detective Service. Your little picture goes right here, pointing to the center of the badge."

Marcia examined the brass plated badge, the pleated leaves surrounding it, and a crevice for the picture. She sat back in her chair.

"And where do I get a picture?"

"Thought you'd never ask," Rufus said as he got up with his camera and went over to a computer and printer. He pulled up a bar stool in front of them along with a chair.

"Sit right over here."

Rufus took her picture, modified it on a Photo Software program and printed it onto Kodak paper. He cut it out and inserted it into the badge along with a transparent cover. And then he proudly pinned the badge to her shirt.

"There you go. The first woman employee of Stronger's Detective Service. How's that?"

"Okay. I like it. Do I have to wear it all the time?"

"No. Just when you need to show your I.D., like when a policeman asks for it. You do need to wear it at the warehouse gate booth."

Rufus walked back over to his desk and sat down. "I've scheduled you for a firearms class next Saturday at the academy firing range."

"I have to use a gun?" Marcia asked.

"Be a good idea to have one," Rufus answered. "Just a small .38 caliber."

Rufus opened his bottom drawer and pulled out one to show her.

"It doesn't look dangerous," Marcia said.

"No. Not until the trigger is pulled," Rufus smirked. "We'll see how it goes. With your looks, you can charm your way out of trouble."

Marcia frowned and realized her situation had not gotten any better with her looks or charm but at least she was trying, and Rufus was being realistic about how the world operated.

"Any questions?" he asked.

"No. Let's get a sandwich and go investigate something," Marcia said.

They both smiled and picked up the items. They started for the door but Rufus stopped and started back.

"Need to show you something," he said as he opened a closet door.

Inside the closet was a lockbox of keys.

"These are alphabetically arranged according to the job; for instance, the Hendricks case, look under the "H" to find keys associated with job; could be a motel room key, car key, or house key.

In this case we need keys for the warehouse and the gate outside. The keys are under "W" for Whitten, the owner.

Rufus grabbed the keys and locked the box. He showed Marcia where he was hiding the key to the lockbox, closed the closet door, and they again headed towards the front door.

After exiting the office, they walked across the street to Rosie's Café and bought a couple sandwiches that had already been made.

Rufus walked Marcia back across the street to his Black Honda SUV in the parking lot behind the building and showed her where to park her car from then on.

"I'll meet you at your car in front of the building and you can follow me to the site," Rufus said. "Fortunately, the site is toward your place and it won't be such a long drive for you to go home tonight."

Marcia got into her car and followed Rufus to a set of old commercial buildings located at the water's edge of the James River. The buildings were constructed of tin roofs and wooden siding. Railroad wood ties were supporting bulkheads and loading dock platforms along the buildings.

Rufus and Marcia exited off the main asphalt road onto a bumpy dirt road that had depressions from heavy rains and water runoff.

Within a minute, Rufus stopped, and Marcia found herself looking at a 40,000 square foot closed building with a large sliding door on caster wheels in front and an 8' high aluminum wire fence surrounding the area with barbed wire on top. The fence was about ten yards away from the perimeter of the building – at the water's edge.

"Must be high tide," Marcia jokingly said to herself. "Looks like a prison."

Rufus had parked off to the side of the entrance near the gated fence which had a booth fronting it. He got out of the vehicle and stood outside the booth and stared at it as Marcia approached him.

He said, "Well, this is it." And he looked at Marcia for a response.

"Could be worse, like out in the water I suppose."

"It looks drab, but the money for this job is good." Rufus said, as he smiled and lifted his eyebrows."

"How good?" Marcia asked.

"Good enough. We monitor this place in the evenings and verify comings and goings. The manager says he will give me $400/night which isn't bad for hanging around 8 hours. Whaddya think?"

"How much are you paying me anyway Rufus? We haven't discussed that."

"We haven't discussed a lot of things. Well, I don't know. How much are you worth?" Rufus said, as he waited for that to sink in but Marcia said nothing.

He looked around the area momentarily to see a tractor trailer rig slowly making its way to a loading dock at the back of a building down the road. "I mean you're new at this."

Marcia thought about it, "Well I promise to do a good job and make sure the place is secure and verify the right people are going in and out."

"Tell you what. Let's see how the first week goes, and if everything goes okay, we divide it 60-40, my 60 of course."

"Fair enough partner. Now when do I get my gun?"

Rufus laughed and said, "Saturday at the range!"

21.

The booth had a heater, overhead light, receptacle outlet, stool, and a convex mirror that looked at the building's front wall and entrance.

Rufus looked around the perimeter and saw nothing unusual. A few shorebirds were foraging for food on the mud banks in the shadows, and a lone cormorant was on the top of a boulder gazing at the water.

He walked around to the opposite side of the warehouse and saw nothing but cattails and some wild oats growing at the water's edge. A 14' wooden boat filled with commercial crab traps and a single occupant was motoring from red float to red float to retrieve large wired metal crab traps from this side of the river. The man would stop at a float and stick out a curled rod to retrieve a waterborne line. He'd pull a trap up to the side of the boat and lift it over the side.

Then he'd unlock the trap's door and dump the crabs in a wooden bucket, which he covered with a wet towel.

Rufus walked back to the booth and unlocked the door to find a manifest of the week's activities.

Two people named Graemes and Ortegan would arrive at the compound around 3:00. They would stay there most of the evening but might leave for a couple hours and come back, and then leave for good at 10:00 p.m., when the compound was to be secured and locked up.

Marcia was gazing at some lilies on a dirt mound when Rufus called her over.

"This job is basically a security job. No one goes in or out except these three guys on the manifest. That's it."

"What if a stranger wants in?"

"Shoot him!"

"I don't have a gun."

Richie shook his head and reached behind his shirt to retrieve a pistol and said, "Here, take mine." And he laid the .38 caliber pistol on the desk in the booth.

Marcia looked at it and looked back at Rufus.

She looked squeamish and said, "I've never picked up a gun. There was never one around the house because mom thought that dad would get drunk and kill us."

"Well, lesson number one is to pick it up with the barrel pointing away."

Marcia picked it up with both hands when Rufus stopped her. "Use one hand and pick it up by the handle."

Marcia picked it up swinging the barrel toward Rufus and Rufus ducked out of the booth.

"Oh, okay. I got it now," yelled Marcia. "Now what?" Marcia asked.

"Now put it back down," and she was wise enough this time to make sure the barrel was pointing towards the back of the booth.

Rufus picked it back up and stood beside Marcia and opened the cylinder. He showed her the bullets, and then he rotated the cylinder a couple times and gave it back to her.

She did the same. "Okay, I like it, and it can fit in my pocket."

"No, no," Rufus said. "You need a holster, but for tonight, just keep it in the booth hidden in case you need it."

"So this thing is ready to shoot when I close the cylinder?" Marcia asked.

"Yes, when a bullet is in the chamber, it's ready. All you do is pull the trigger."

"Let's try it."

Rufus smirked a little and looked around and saw no one. "Okay, let's go over near the mud bank so the sound won't travel as far."

Seeing nothing near the bank and in the background of the river, he said, "Now use two hands without a finger on the trigger and take a stance square to a target. Aim at that concrete boulder over there," he said, pointing near the water's edge.

Marcia turned towards the target, spread her legs shoulder length, and pointed the gun toward the water.

"Good. Now do it again and aim at that single railroad tie lying in the mud. Aim through the end sight of the gun to the target, and hold it for a second. Make sure you're shooting arm is straight out toward the target. Hold the gun firm and pull the trigger."

Marcia crouched a bit like in the movies and brought the gun up with two hands and sighted down the barrel. She found the trigger with her right index finger and pulled it back and the gun fired and jerked her hands back; she felt the reverberation through her body. And she felt a calm.

She closed her eyes for a second while smoke lingered in the air with her ears ringing. She brushed her hair back and regained her composure.

"Did I hit it?" she asked.

"You hit something. It was a little high and to the right but not bad. Always figure when you pull the trigger there's a tendency to pull it right, so compensate. But for now, that's enough. You did well. Pull the cylinder open and unload the bullets."

Marcia figured that out, and knowing the gun was unloaded, jammed it in her pants at her hip like a cowboy and gave Rufus a confident nod. She put the bullets in her pocket.

He shook his head. "Wow. Okay, I got to be going. Call me tomorrow."

He left with Marcia still a little shell shocked and looking for the mark of the bullet in the mud.

Pretty good this investigative work, she thought. And then she felt some unnatural pain. *Uh, oh, these people know I'm here and I hope they don't hurt me.*

She headed to the booth looking for a cap or something to shield her head. She remembered there was one in her bag, so she reached in and got it and put it on.

It helped some but she still felt vulnerable. From what Naomi said about this radar stuff, some foil would help block the energy. Looking on the floor, Marcia saw a chewing gum wrapper, bent down and picked it up and put it in her hat.

Again, she felt a little better, and she thanked God for Naomi.

Rufus did a U-turn and came back to yell out his Toyota's window, "Almost forgot. Lock the gate after those two guys go in and tuck the key away safely until they want out. Anyone else comes around; tell them to talk to the manager of the facility. His card is in the booth. Okay?"

"Sure, but this all seems hush-hush to me and rather devious."

"Well, do a little investigating but don't get yourself killed, and if you want to know the truth, that's partly why we're here. No more questions."

"Wow, the boss has spoken. Hey, where do I eat?"

"Right here. Call out for something or bring something next time. Now have a great night and if anything crazy happens, try to handle it. I'm surveying deliveries of fake goods at a building downtown. I'll be there until 7: 00 in the morning, so call me in the afternoon."

"Okay boss. When do I get paid again?"

"Friday afternoon, if you're good!" Rufus yelled from the vehicle as he left.

And Marcia sat on the stool thinking about things. *Jeez, $160 a night for sitting here is something I think I could live with.*

22.

Thirty miles away on the other side of the Hampton Roads Bridge Tunnel in Virginia Beach, Schmidt Rossier was sitting in the Heron Inn Restaurant overlooking the mouth of the Chesapeake Bay for a cargo freighter which would dock at the Norfolk International port terminal at 9:00 p.m.

He was nervous. His hands were shaking -- knowing that this could be the last time he had freedom.

If he ever got caught doing what he was doing, jail time would be for life.

It was now 2:00.

Rossier looked around the Inn to see if anyone had followed him but there were no other people at the tables at this hour. There was an unobstructed view inside the Inn and to the beach outside.

The Heron Inn was a perfect place to watch a ship leaving or arriving at the bay because it was located just inside the bay's mouth at Lynnhaven Inlet.

The Inn had been built in 1945 during World War II, when the Navy offered contracts for shipbuilding in the Tidewater area and a host of people migrated to the area to find jobs and recreation.

The Inn started out as a clapboard pilots' house, but two storms crashed the beach in the next two decades and left it in ruins.

It was rebuilt each time, with added metal supports in the sand and pier posts three feet above ground.

Since then, it had withstood the strong northeastern storms off the Atlantic Ocean: overflowing waters would simply go underneath the Inn and recede back within hours.

Finally, the owners felt secure enough to make the house into a restaurant and decorate the Inn's walls and decking.

Fish nets were hung from the walls and draped over some of the eating tables. Sun weathered life jackets hung over oak storage barrels. Enameled crab, mussel, and clam shells were intertwined in nylon fishing nets that were hung on the walls.

There were pictures of record sized fish and a stuffed blue marlin on one wall. The floor was made of pine planks, and the exterior off the Inn had been lapped with cement boards to withstand the worst wind storms.

100 yards away at the mouth of the Lynnhaven Inlet, a lone fisherman was casting a line out to the side of the current hoping to catch a trout.

There had always been a strong current at the 50 yard inlet; a number of people had drowned there. Numbers of total drowning victims each year would be posted on a sign above the inlet on a bridge support piling – giving people a fair warning of the danger.

Many people thought they could swim across the inlet, only to be carried one way or another to deeper water. Others thought they could tip toe across the large boulders, which acted as a bulkhead under the bridge, only to slip on the moss laden rocks and fall into the water and not get back to shore.

It was a clear day, and Rossier kept his eyes peeled for an orange hulled freighter entering the bay area with a reflection signal from a mirror lens which would tell him a load of goods would be dropped off at the same location as last time -- on the Hampton Roads channel side of the bay just past the Bay Bridge tunnel off to the north side of the freighter. That would help shield anyone from taking pictures of the drop from beach front homes.

Rossier would navigate his 21' boat skiff and retrieve 500 pounds of heroin worth over $1,000,000,000 in 10 bundles that weighed 50 pounds each with 22 brick packages – that was wrapped with plastic and reinforced polyvinyl chloride rubber and tied together with 12 gauge aluminum wire.

The packages would float on the water by air-filled canvas tubing. Two transmitters and a small beacon light accompanied each load. If the seas were rough, Rossier would have to wait a couple days and the load would be picked up from the sea bottom further up the bay outside the strong tidal current -- without the floatation material.

But today was good weather, and the four light signal had been sent five times just after a 4:00 p.m. entrance of the freighter into the bay's mouth.

Rossier got up from his chair and paid the bill for the shrimp basket and beer at the cashier's stand. He exited the restaurant and drove his car around the corner to a marina on the inlet's side.

The 100,000 ton cargo freighter from Entebbe was moving at 5 knots and likely to be at the drop off point in two hours.

Rossier had plenty of time: it was only a fifteen minute trip to the location.

His boat was gassed and ready. A prong hook for retrieving the drop lines was available. Fishing tackle and poles were in place for his excuse if questioned, and the boat's running lights worked fine.

He grabbed a raincoat, pair of boots, and gloves out of his vehicle and boarded the boat. He cranked up the two Mercury 75 horsepower engines and untied the boat's restraining ropes from the dock's poles, and he drove the boat out of the inlet and into the bay.

It was going to be an easy run with the tide ebbing and the wind at his back to slow the current flow.

He motored west along the beach and anchored 1000 yards offshore. He grabbed a fishing pole and cast a baitless hook into the water.

23.

Brahaim was sitting in his bunker at Bougainville looking at Marcia on his computer while she was in the booth at the Newport News warehouse. He wondered if the targeting suppressed her but there were no unorthodox movements from her: she was just sitting there reading a book.

He didn't want to hurt anyone in this job, but being a poor farmer in Yemen wasn't fun either, so he volunteered to do this work. If he had not taken it, his family was sure to be terrorized at home.

"Well, everything is going well Tori," he said.

Tori had just arrived to take over monitoring Cell 1's activities for the next eight hours. After that, The Premiere would take over.

This last of the month shipment of drugs by the freighter would be made tonight at the warehouse by Rossier and his boat, but this same action was happening to other locations scattered around the world.

Twenty billion dollars of drugs flowed from the Middle East and South America every month outside of United States drug enforcement agencies with Zenithe's system.

The District of Columbia corridor to Norfolk was a prime market because of government defense money and its receivers.

The organization had three missions: make money, get people addicted to drugs, and control the populace.

The organization not only made money from covert drug sales but from the medical industry when victims went to doctors and psychiatrists, whom mailed monthly dues to a shell organization of medical employees.

Zenithe had personnel in medical, law enforcement, and insurance organizations working for them.

Tori glanced at the monitor and saw split screen images of the freighter, Marcia's booth, and Rossier, who was sitting on his boat fishing.

The bay was cleared of most boat traffic with energy fields by another computer program. Rossier would have a clear rim to the dock at the warehouse.

"She'll be alright tonight but eventually she'll get curious about what's in the warehouse. Let's see how she reacts a night or two," Brahaim said to Tori.

He left the building and went down a jungle path to a mining camp that had a bunkhouse.

Tori took a walk to look at other monitors and activities. He saw no warning bells that some fool was exceeding his DNA potential or blocking the targeting and becoming out of line.

24.

Marcia got up from the stool in the booth and walked outside to become familiar with the area.

Warehouses lined the banks of the James River and there was a fishing pier jutting out from the shore on its opposite side.

From the booth, two roads led away to more warehouses which looked empty and deserted.

She walked around the perimeter fence to a bulkhead at the water's edge. It was five foot tall and held the bank of the ground in place with salt treated lumber topped with crushed stone. The water below was muddy looking and teeming with small minnows swimming along the edge. The water was ebbing outward, and the area smelled of sulfur from leftover debris and salt residue.

There was a thick humid fog at the water's edge where night met day.

She went to the other side of the compound and saw the same except for the words on the side of the warehouse said, Jamin's Express, which caught her attention.

Maybe it was an old trucking company repair shop or something? She thought.

She walked back to the booth sidestepping fiddler crabs and keeping her balance along the ruts in the ground.

She looked at the manifest board on the wall and memorized the names on the sheet.

Twenty minutes later Graemes and Ortegan drove up to the gate in a white paneled truck with darkened front windows with the horn honking.

Graemes lowered his window and looked at Marcia without saying a word.

She brought the clipboard with the manifest sheet towards him and turned slightly so that he could see her I.D. badge under her dark blue nylon shell vest. She was proud of it, and she asked the men for identification.

Graemes, with his black hair and sweaty dark weathered face, grimaced, but reached in his back pocket and took out a Virginia driver's license from his wallet.

Ortegan did the same, and handed his to Graemes.

Both men looked Latin American with their tanned faces, black hair, and multi-colored shirts.

Graemes handed both I.D.s through the window to Marcia, who verified the names and the pictures beside the names on the manifest. Everything matched, and Marcia gave the I.D.s back.

She unlocked the gate padlock, and it took all her strength to push the large gate along.

The steel wheel casters under the gate were dirty and rusty. but finally the gate slid along its track which allowed the truck to enter the compound; then she slid the gate back and locked them in.

Graemes and Ortegan drove up to the warehouse and unlocked a padlock and swung the large door back for the truck to enter.

Once inside, they made sure everything was as they left it: weighing scales, plastic bags of various sizes, and boxes of corn starch, with which they would dilute the drug cakes.

All the items were under a black plastic tarp behind oil drums, a hydraulic lift, and tractor trailer tarps.

And the shipping labels that said, All-Dri – The Best Natural Absorbent For Any Spill -- were in a box above it all.

25.

As Rossier sat just offshore with his fishing pole, he looked off in the distance to see the freighter approaching the Hampton Roads channel.

He reeled in the fishing line and put the pole in its holder and pulled up anchor.

He started the engines and motored to get just ahead of the freighter so when it passed he would not be swamped by the wake of water that would rush by the broadside of the boat.

He wanted to angle the boat forward into the waves to cut through the swells and not be overturned into channel's rushing water.

He slowed and let the tide take him out slowly, while he again cast out the fishing line.

He was sure the captain knew about this drug drop, otherwise the captain would be complaining about a fisherman in the channel.

Rossier found himself in this drug running operation years earlier while in the Navy overseas and taking a vacation in Cape Town, South Africa.

He hooked up with a supplier, shipped some drugs to the United States and made good money. He had also brought some of the heroin in his duffle bag back to the U.S. when on leave from the Navy.

Knowing the heroin was good quality, because his customers were pleased, he started importing the drug by worker friends at the International Port docks when the Postal Service started inspecting packages over one pound.

His contact in South Africa had acquired the drugs from Afghanistan, where a ship would take a southern route to unload it at Cape Town.

Derived from morphine, from the unripe seeds of opium poppy, heroin would be cut with inert ingredients and sold in plastic bags to military personnel such as Rossier, who had little to do but smoke marijuana and use drugs on the ship.

Eventually, he gave up using the drug after experiencing health problems, but he would not give up making the money. He had hoped the drug was being put to good use but deep down in his heart, he knew it wasn't.

When the freighter neared, Rossier got ready for one of the bigger waves coming and turned his boat straight through it. After a series of smaller waves, he slowed and leaned against the far railing of the boat and waited.

He saw a red bundle drop alongside the rear of the ship that blended in with ship's paint but when it hit the water turned a watery green color as the red disappeared into the air.

These guys think of everything, he thought.

He waited a few minutes while watching the light blue flotation blocks and trying to gauge their movement with the tide.

He looked around to see little activity on the bay; there was only one sailboat edging along the beach.

Drifting nearer the drop, he stuck his fishing pole in the trolling position and motored over to the floating gold. He measured the running tide and fell in with movement of the blocks, with any shore people blocked from watching the boat by the big freighter: he got his prong hook out and grabbed the wire stringer and slowly retrieved each block from the water. Occasionally he would pick up his fishing pole and act like he was fishing.

He put each pack in the middle of the boat and put a black canvas tarp over them.

He slowly turned the boat towards shore acting as if he were trolling for fish. After a couple of minutes, he wound in the fishing line and turned the boat west towards Newport News and the James River.

He stayed close to the southern shore where the water was calm and the outgoing tide slower.

Lights began to glitter from condominiums at Chick's beach and Ocean View as the sun began to set and darkness covered the beaches.

Then he turned northward across the Hampton Roads Tunnel and into the mouth of the James River.

It took him about 40 minutes to make the trip.

It was 7:00 p.m. when he approached the warehouse on Waterfront Road in Newport News.

Seeing the big white Jamin's Express letters on the side of the building, Rossier swung the boat to the middle of the river and approached the warehouse perpendicular to shore so any noise from the motor would be less likely to be heard on land.

A back door of the building topped the bulkhead's platform and a blue light bulb was on.

He backed off the throttle and let the motion of the boat carry him to the bulkhead. Due to some strategic dredging, there was plenty of water here for the boat to tie up alongside the 5' bulkhead platform.

Graemes and Ortegan were sitting just inside the doorway playing cards when they had heard the sound of the motors minutes earlier.

They opened the door and waited as Rossier drifted in and threw a rope to the top of the platform, where Ortegan grabbed it and tied it to a cleat.

Rossier threw the tarp off the packages and lifted up each package from the boat and onto pier planks.

Ortegan knew when the freighter had entered the bay because he was tracking it via his telephone internet service. And he knew Rossier would not have had time to cut the drug on the trip to the warehouse: there was no reason to check its purity again or open the packs.

The three men got the packages inside the warehouse and gave sighs of relief. No one seemed to follow Rossier.

Graemes gave Rossier $2,000 and told him to come back tomorrow for his share to distribute.

Rossier nodded and looked over the water at the back door for any Port Police.

He jumped down into the boat and engaged the starter and backed away from the bulkhead. The tide would be coming in soon, and the faster he got going, the easier the trip would be back to the marina. At least the wind would be calm now as the sun had set and the ocean calmed.

Graemes and Ortegan retrieved a small dolly and put the packages on it and took them to the truck. Tomorrow they would bring the packages back and dilute them each to 25% purity.

At 9:45, they drove out of the warehouse and stopped briefly to lock the garage door; then they gave Marcia a beep from the horn signaling they were ready to exit the compound.

She was sitting in the booth reading a book about a woman detective and her husband policeman who saved her from getting murdered by a drug cartel when he showed up with two armed buddies and captured the dealers. *Gee, I don't want anything like that,* she thought. *I don't have a policeman husband anyway.*

But Marcia knew the men were leaving when they had closed to the door to the warehouse; she never heard or saw any boat; and she didn't know there was water access at the back of the warehouse.

But she did wonder what was in the warehouse, and she looked curiously at the truck as it slowly stopped at the gate.

She took her time opening the gate while looking for any clue to help her figure out the mystery.

She thought a little charm might help, so she walked a little straighter and gave a smile to Ortegan and let some hair hang sway on the way around the truck.

The men stared, while Marcia noticed a state inspection sticker on the windshield and the station that applied it, the license number of the truck, and what looked to be a little salt water under the rear door panel as she walked around the truck.

Tomorrow she would find out why.

She went and opened the front gate and gave them a nod to pass through while continuing to smile. *Nothing like God's love to reveal matters*, she thought.

The truck drove through and she pushed the gate back and locked it.

Nothing seemed to bother her too much here at the booth, but what about when she got home. She would wonder. Had someone been in her apartment again while she was working?

She stepped back into the booth and looked to make sure the one window was locked. There wasn't anything valuable in the booth but a heat pump air conditioner heater unit fitted into a wall. She locked the door.

As she stepped out into the parking lot, a small light caught her attention from a mini-storage facility 75 yards away off across the dirt road off to the side. If it hadn't bothered her eyes at that moment, she wouldn't have thought anything of it.

But Naomi had also mentioned being bothered by lights– and said something about radiological frequencies harming people.

Marcia shined her high beam flashlight to that area but all she saw were vacant storage units, and the office.

She was looking for anyone in the vicinity.

There was nothing, so she got in her car and drove towards home, still bothered by what had happened. She had a lot to learn about this investigating business.

Everything was quiet at her apartment building. and most residents have their lights off. There were street lamps on but they were the incandescent ones that did not seem to bother her.

She drove into the parking lot and got out of the car with her bag.

It wasn't much of a place but still home for now. Management kept it up well by painting regularly, changing air filters, and mowing the grass outside. And she liked her neighbors – two older people next door.

She got to the door and everything looked the same as she had left it: the markers put between the jamb and the door top were still there, the stick that was put behind the door was in the same place before it was fully opened; and there were no strange smells, or dirt on the floor.

She walked inside, closed the door, and locked it.

She went over to her message machine and saw two messages: one was a hang-up and the other was from Richie saying hi. She'd call him tomorrow like she promised. She put her bags down and went to dress down for bed. She turned off all the lights, lay down and began to pray for safety and wisdom.

She remembered Naomi saying earplugs and headphones often worked to keep out unwanted noise or voices. But Marcia thought that to be a trap – because then a person couldn't hear what was going on around the area.

After prayers, she put a pillow over her head and went to sleep.

While Marcia was sleeping, Premiere was in Bougainville closely watching Rossier's movements. The heroin was safely in Graemes' vehicle, and Rossier was heading back home to Virginia Beach.

On another monitor, Rufus Stronger was preparing for his night shift to keep Andy Whitten's building under surveillance.

Paneled trucks from another operation would soon be arriving with Zenithe's misbranded goods.

And yet another screen showed Ortegan and Graemes leaving a bar and going home after having a couple of beers. *Idiots. They're all idiots,* the Premiere was thinking.

Once this end of this month's transaction was completed, Premiere could rest by engaging an artificial intelligence program on the whole group of them.

Timing was the key to make all these events happen, because the programming of each action was dependent on the weather being manipulated with chemical spraying by the military at the end of the month, facilitating the remote control programs operating through the electrical grid and cell phone towers – and then there was the money factor – when the government released funds at the end of the month for Zenithe's buyers.

If part of the system failed, the organization had law enforcement officials, lawyers, and politicians who had been paid off to protect the organization's interests.

But Premiere continued to worry about Marcia. She was learning fast about the system and difficult to control at times. She went places that the system had not showed her, and said things the system had not pulsed.

And she had that boyfriend lawyer who could cause trouble for Skooly.

Premiere walked away from the monitors and looked through the window at the light of a waxing moon over the ocean.

The organization wouldn't like anything happening out of the ordinary to Cell 1, and he knew it would cost him dearly.

Communications out of the bunker were to be kept to a minimum but there were times he had to talk to Skooly, if anything just to be assured the old man had everything under control

So he punched in Skooly's phone number on a cell phone.

"Yes," Skooly said as he answered the phone.

"How are you?" Premiere asked.

"Something amiss Johnny?" Skooly questioned using Premiere's nickname and ignoring the question.

"No. No. But the girl worries me at times," he responded.

"What did she do?"

"She could figure it all out."

"Don't worry. Julian can take care of it, and probably already has," Skooly responded.

"Okay. Okay. It's just that this one's different with the boyfriend and all."

"The judge can take care of that too," Skooly said.

Johnny wasn't getting the answers he wanted and started pacing the floor with his phone at his ear.

"These new victims are figuring out what we're doing! They're not dumb. They use magnets to deflect electro-magnetic field controls, reflective mirrors to redirect light, and all kinds of stuff! Some of those implants that were put in them are being disabled!"

"Calm down. The system is secure. They can only get so far and the system takes over," answered Skooly.

A calm took place on the phone that left each man thinking.

Finally Skooly said, ""You thinking of leaving?"

Johnny said, "You know what the outcome would be. There's one other thing. Someone knows where we're at."

"Who?"

"I don't know but we're receiving computer warnings that someone is locking onto our communications."

"Well, you got guards around the perimeter of the island and a program that self-destructs. You got a birthday cake for me?"

"On the way," answered the Premiere.

"Good night and don't worry. The organization has been around a long time and it's not going anywhere."

And Skooly hung up his landline phone.

Premiere walked away from his desk in the bunker and wondered why he was doing what he was doing. The only answer he could get was that he was doing it for the fathers, fathers of whom had suffered much in the past and would not let anyone ever control them.

But this targeting system was more than self-defense: it was gregarious and tortuous. And Johnny remembered in history when his people had become odious and despicable in the sight of other nations, and God sent an army to destroy them. There would be a price to pay.

26.

Rossier woke up with some terrible feelings.

After all, yesterday he had delivered enough heroin from a ship to put him in jail for life. Plus, he was a distributor for the southern Tidewater area after the heroin was cut.

Tonight he would drive to the warehouse at Newport News and pick up a bundle of 23 bricks that will have been diluted and repackaged in smaller bags for sale to dealers and individuals: mostly Navy seaman.

Rossier lived in a 2-story one bedroom townhouse that had a garage on the bottom floor.

To make sure everything was in order and not get stopped by the police, Rossier went down into the garage and checked the Toyota SUV's lights to make sure they were working. He checked the tires, wipers, and seat belts. The last thing he needed was for his vehicle to get stopped.

And then he checked that his registration and insurance form was in the glove compartment. He made sure his driver's license was in his wallet.

He went back upstairs and sat at the kitchen table nervous about the pick-up tonight. Ortegan had told him there was a new person at the gate.

A three cushion sofa covered with green rayon fabric sat in front of a wood coffee table in the living room. Rossier went over to it and laid down, the whole time seeing images of jail walls and prison guards. He didn't know if he was dreaming or it was real after a few minutes, so he walked back into the kitchen and got a glass of water to clear his head.

Maybe this it, the end, he was thinking.

He looked over at pictures of his Navy days that lined the walls: there were pictures of ships, friends, and foreign ports. Those were good days, happy times, and now he was in some kind of situation he had not fully figured how to get out of.

He wouldn't be in this situation long after making this kind of money every month.

He fixed a cup of instant coffee, sat down on a bar stool, and relaxed. And then he thought about one thing he had forgotten to pack – his gun – just in case there was trouble.

He thought about rush hour and how the roads were busy around 5:00 p.m. with Naval Base workers getting off from work, so he decided to leave around 3:00 and get to Newport News at 4:00. Graemes and Ortegan should be there by then and have the packages ready. He had already been there three times this year.

The only thing he wasn't sure about was the new guard at the gate. Every week it seemed there was a new guard, so this was an unknown factor. He would wear his sunglasses, hat, and a high collar to hide much of his face, and he didn't plan on getting out of the vehicle.

27.

Marcia woke up with the sun shining in the room but she was still tired.

She used the bathroom and walked to the living room and sat on the couch thinking about things.

A song repeated in her mind for awhile that she had not heard for years; she knew right then it wasn't something she was voluntarily singing.

How great is this to at least know it's not me! She thought.

Was there a receiver in here somewhere? She asked herself. *Or maybe her metal cavity fillings were picking up signals?*

But if the foil Naomi suggested works at times, the signal was being interrupted.

All these thoughts were going through her mind when she thought about eating something, because she had to work tonight.

She fixed some boiled eggs, oats, and a couple pieces of sausage. She ate and laid back down drifting off to sleep on the couch.

Shortly after 10:00, she got up and decided to take the garbage to the dumpster and also have a look around the complex. Someone had to be nearby watching her because they were able to get to her place quickly and get out. She had been to the store down the street on numerous occasions and been gone for only 20 minutes; yet someone had been in her apartment with muddy shoes on the floor. That fast.

Her car looked fine, but it had many times before, only to find out someone had taken her sunglasses, readjusted her mirror, or moved her seat back, just anything to make her think she was going crazy.

She was supposed to complain to the police about every little incident to make her look crazy, but that would make her look crazy, so she never bothered.

And then she thought about Skooly. He was the only one to profit from her going crazy – saying she didn't know what she was talking about if someone prosecuted Skooly's legal team for targeting their own clients to make them sick and make money off state compensation claims.

It always got back to Skooly, an old established lawyer whom many a client complained about overcharging and filing vain papers. And then it struck her that Skooly was likely using one of his own clients to stalk her. She would need to find a list of his clients somehow.

She went back to her apartment and thought about last night. She enjoyed the job, and now that she saw that water oozing from the back of the truck, it pricked her investigative mind to find out where it was coming from.

She had some tea, smiled at her confidence to have a job and be somewhat happy -- out of an office atmosphere. She was free, and wherever fate led her is where she would end up.

She figured Rufus to have gotten some rest by now, so she picked up the phone and gave him a call.

He answered on the fourth ring.

"Good morning from your associate," Marcia said.

"Oh. Sounds like you made it through the night," he answered.

"Me and the crickets, and the small fiddler crabs scavenging over the rocks around the booth. How's your job?"

"Nothing. That's the way it goes sometimes. But what is not seen is evidence too, which reminds me, always keep a log of anything that happens on your shift. Graemes and Ortegan come in: log it in that journal in the bottom drawer of the desk. Just anything that seems important," Rufus said.

"How about water escaping from the back of their truck bed?"

"Excuse me?" Rufus inquired.

"There was water leaking from under the back pull down door and onto the ground when the truck was leaving last night," Marcia responded.

"Well, was it there when they went in the gate earlier?"

"Didn't see none, and I would have when the truck passed the gate," Marcia said.

"Maybe they had a cooler of drinks in the back and some ice fell out when they opened it. Could've been anything," Rufus responded.

"Maybe. Could have been ice on a dead body from the way those two look. They left about 9:45 and then I took off. What's the light shining across the way?"

"Storage facility office probably. People come and go but mostly in daylight hours, though I have seen activity at night.'

"Okay, just thought I'd ask. Well, time to get ready for work. Again, thanks so much for the job Rufus. I like it," Marcia finished.

"You're welcome. Let me know where that water is coming from. Hey, maybe they went fishing outside?"

"Now how would they do that?" Marcia asked.

"I think there's a back door, or at least Andy referred to the structure having water access."

"A back door? To the warehouse that fronts the water?" Marcia asked.

"That's what I've heard. See if you can figure that out, and I'll see if we're responsible to secure it."

"I'll figure out something if I have to get in a boat. I want to be an investigator and solve my problems too."

"Don't we all. Talk tomorrow wonder woman."

133

"Bye," Marcia said, and she hung up the phone.

A back door, someone dropped something off that had water in it? Marcia thought.

Marcia sat for awhile continuing to think about that back door but also her home situation. She got up and started cleaning and clearing out anything that did not belong in the apartment. She wanted to know if anyone was coming in and changing things or taking them.

It was 12: 30 and Richie should be on his lunch hour, so she called.

He answered immediately, "Hey investigator."

"How are you doing?"

"Okay." He knew Marcia would keep his actions confidential, so he talked about his morning's work: "I filed a claim against Grand Bicycle for $100,000 for pain and suffering and asked for $50,000 in punitive damages."

"Not a big case then huh?" Marcia questioned.

"Not big for one kid but there are others out there who've had problems with the same metal bar producer," Richie responded.

"I see. One thing may lead to another, and you could set the standard for bicycle frame assembly."

"Something like that. But it's not the monetary awards for the victims that so much matters: it's the companies neglecting the safety of consumers by cutting corners to make more money. And yes, it could snowball into a class action lawsuit including multiple plaintiffs and I would be a top notch bicycle claims attorney."

"Wow. That sounds important! Would you be my attorney if I fell off a bicycle?"

"Depends on the cause. You pedal and steer right?"

"Would I lead you wrong?" Marcia asked.

"No."

"Okay then. Can we get together for lunch tomorrow at noon?"

"Name the place," Richie asked.

"Oh, let's get a sandwich at Jean's Deli over there near you."

"It's a date. I want to hear about your job and Stronger."

"Stronger is Stronger: down to earth, business like and a macho guy. Don't hand him a pistol barrel pointed at him though."

Richie laughed. "No. Always point it down and away. Okay. See you at noon."

"Bye."

28.

Marcia got up from the couch and went into the kitchen to fix a tuna fish sandwich – out of a can and from some crackers she knew were safe from drugging.

Tonight she would be prepared for anything that looked suspicious around the warehouse.

She'd bring a camera with a 10x zoom lens and a voice activated tape recorder. She'd try to get some kind of a picture of the storage facility adjacent to the warehouse, and if anyone came by the booth and threatened her, the recorder would pick up the conversation.

To occupy her free time, she would pack a puzzle book and the detective novel. She would get a couple of canned goods, bottle of water, and some plastic ware from the cabinets for her dinner. *May as well enjoy the time*, she thought. And she'd stick a chocolate bar in the bag.

Maybe this job would get her into a real investigator's job.

She got up and gathered all the provisions and put them in a back pack along with the small pistol Rufus had given her. She went to the bedroom and again dressed in navy blue and black. She brushed her hair straight back and put a couple of clips on the sides. She also got some lotion for her face and arms to protect her from the bugs and scum that seemed to be coming off the water from a nearby marine terminal and passing boats. She packed some gloves to protect her hands from moving that heavy fence gate.

Packed and ready, she went to the kitchen and hid some of her important food in case the perpetrators came in tonight. A bottle was slid in front of the refrigerator door as a marker; other foods were covered with clothes. *If they're going to drug something, may as well make them work for it,* she thought.

Before she closed the front door, she stuck her markers in the jamb and went to the car looking all around for some evidence of who was harassing her.

Seeing no prints on the door handle, she opened the door and got in. Then she noticed the ash tray was opened, and she knew she didn't do it. And so the mystery of targeting continued.

But she was becoming more assured each day that her adversary would be caught. The wheels of justice and manifestation were turning.

She would also talk to her good neighbors and ask them to be on the lookout for any strange people at the complex – to make sure any visitor be registered at the rental office.

She would learn how to fingerprint, take close-up pictures, and call the right person when she needed information. She needed that investigator's license, but Stronger would have to do for now.

She got to work at 2: 00 and found everything secure. There were no new tread marks on the driveway and no one visible at the storage facility.

She unloaded her gear in the booth and took a walk to the water's edge to see if there was a back door to the warehouse, but the angle from the cattail weeded area to the back prohibited it.

She wanted to see it the back of the warehouse, so she went back to the booth and got a make-up mirror and taped it to a pole and stuck it out over the weeds to try and take a picture of the mirror.

That was too hard to see six feet away and the mirror only reflected so much of its area.

Then she noticed the shoreline angled away from the door towards the river, if only she would walk 100 yards down the edge of the weeds. She took her camera and trudged along the gravel filled embankment walking over more drainage ruts and washed up oyster shells.

When she was able to see the back of the warehouse, she took the camera lens cover off, turned on the camera and opened the f-stop wide as possible and set a high shutter speed.

And there it was, perfectly visible in the southern sun's afternoon light over the river.

She took a couple of pictures on this manual setting and a couple more on the sunset and automatic settings.

When she got back to the booth, she reviewed the pictures and magnified them to see a tin door with an exterior light on the side of its jamb.

Now if she could just find out what had been unloaded from the boat.

She called Stronger and told him the news.

Rufus, still a little tired from his early morning surveillance at Whitten's building, answered the phone, "Rufus, there is a door at the rear."

"Okay. See anyone around?"

"No. But I'll be looking from now on. Who'd you say to call if there was trouble?"

"Well, besides me, call Tellis at the police station, 828-898-2002. He's in charge, but don't do anything stupid. How about us discussing it first?"

"Sure Rufus, as long as there is time."

"Make time," Rufus answered. And Rufus terminated the call and went back to napping.

29.

Graemes and Ortegan arrived at the warehouse at 3:00 and went through the same process as they did the previous day showing their I.D.'s to Marcia.

They got into the building and began to open the drug packages and add mixtures of corn and wheat flour to each batch of heroin. They could easily get four new packages out of one block and sell it to major dealers in Washington, Richmond, and the Tidewater area.

Bougainville was watching the whole scene on its computers, especially Marcia's every move -- with remote sensing applications and an audible alarm that would be activated in the bunker whenever Marcia was 100 yards from her perimeter at the gated warehouse.

Tori went over to check the alarm's activation status.

Knew she was going to be trouble, he thought, *but the drugs have been delivered so there's nothing there. She will figure it out though.*

He didn't see a reason to call anyone so he let it go, but he still thought about Rossier making today's personal pick-up.

And Rossier was getting ready to do just that.

Today he would wear a blue golf shirt, khaki long pants, and a dark brown cap.

At home, Rossier went into his living room closet to retrieve a duffel bag. He turned off the kitchen light, set the burglar alarm, and went down the stairs to his vehicle.

He took his time, again making sure the lights, tires, engine oil, and radiator water levels were all okay. He was nervous and tripped over a concrete pad when walking around the vehicle. After opening the garage door, he looked around to see if any neighbors were watching.

He drove out of the neighborhood and turned left onto Shore Drive and followed it to Northampton Boulevard where he merged onto I-64 North to Newport News.

As he approached the bridge tunnel, he looked out over the bay to see thunderstorm clouds forming. He was glad it was today and not last night when he was boating.

He exited I-64 to Chesapeake St and turned off on a dirt road to the warehouse. He steered his Toyota off to a side road near an empty building and stopped; he reached under the seat and grabbed an old license plate and went to the rear of the vehicle and pinned it over the existing one.

He got back into the vehicle and moved slowly toward the booth and gate.

Marcia had decided she would take a picture of anyone coming or going, or even a boat in the water at the back of the warehouse.

When the vehicle came down the road, her camera was ready and she took a quick picture, then put the camera down on a desk and grabbed the manifest sheet and went to the front gate to meet the truck and check Rossier's I.D.

"You're new," he said, as he gave her his driving license.

"Am. Second day on the job." To test his objective, she asked, "You here for a pickup?"

Rossier was momentarily taken aback as she looked at the manifest sheet.

"Need to talk about some truck parts," he responded.

Marcia checked the information on Rossier's license and said, "Don't got a phone to check truck parts?"

Rossier quickly replied, "Don't got their number."

Marcia ignored the remark and gave him back his identification card and said, "Okay. When you coming back? So I can schedule dinner."

"An hour at the most," Rossier responded.

"See you then," Marcia added. She unlocked the gate and pushed it back looking at the vehicle and getting as much information as possible. When the vehicle was partly through the gate, she quickly went and grabbed the camera off the desk and took a picture. She put the camera into her coat pocket and closed the gate after it went through.

She wrote in a journal: Suspect No. 3. *May as well keep notes like a true investigator. Colombo on TV always wrote stuff down,* she thought.

Rossier beeped his horn a couple of times and Ortegan opened the garage door. Rossier drove into the dark musty smelly building still shaking a little and still wondering about the dream in prison he had. With each trip here, there was more stress.

He got out of the Toyota and told them this was his last trip. He wanted out.

"Sure, sure, sure, man. We'll pass the word and get a replacement," Graemes said.

Without looking up and counting 25 bricks of heroin that had been diluted, he laid two bricks in front of Rossier.

He looked at Rossier for confirmation. Rossier took a pinch and tasted it, nodded okay, and backed off to let them bundle it in All-Dri dark plastic wrap and put it in the vehicle.

He shut the back door and got in the truck.

"Guard asked me if I was here for a pickup," Rossier added.

Graemes and Ortegan looked at each other and shrugged their shoulders.

"She's a pretty woman amigo," Ortegan said.

"Yeah," said Rossier, and he turned the vehicle around in the garage while they opened the door and he headed towards the front gate.

Marcia heard the garage door open before she saw it, and she took another picture to get a glimpse of what was in the warehouse.

She loved her new job! Whereas before she was subject to a judge's orders or the whim of lawyers to record testimonies of criminals, witnesses, and so called experts, now she had control over her situation. Or at least she thought she did, because in the back of her mind someone was still trying to control her.

The vehicle eased out of the garage area towards the front gate. Rossier nodded he was ready to go and pointed towards the street. Before she opened the gate, she wanted to talk to him and asked in a friendly way, "Get what you needed?"

He merely nodded yes and said nothing else. He was spooked enough.

She went and slid the gate sideways to let him out.

Marcia stared intensely as the Toyota passed looking at the license plate that looked a little crooked and wondered about it.

She pushed the gate back towards the booth and went into to the booth and sat. She looked across the street and noticed a little shuffling of feet by someone entering a door over at the storage facility.

He had a tanned face, the vehicle had a trailer hitch – for a boat trailer maybe. The tire treads, I'll get a picture of those now that he's gone.

144

She got her camera and walked over to the trails in the dirt the Toyota had left.

She turned the macro on and got some close-ups of the tire treads on the dirt packed road.

Rossier had stopped a block away, so she zoomed the camera in quickly just as he turned to get another picture of the vehicle. Fortunately, the sun was shining on that side of the vehicle.

This is probably all in vain but it's something to do, she was thinking. *But what I need is to check these names on the manifest -- to check them with the court.*

She thought about all these things and went back to reading her book and eating an apple pie tart.

At 6:00 she ordered a pizza -- and watched the sun set over a placid James River with a few mid-size cargo ships travelling the waters to the marine terminal and south to the Norfolk International Port. A Navy Destroyer was on the far side of the channel heading towards the Atlantic Ocean, and Marcia wondered if there was trouble on the seas.

Her pizza arrived in forty-five minutes, and Marcia wondered why it took so long since the place was only a few blocks away.

After the first bite, she knew why: it was drugged or poisoned. She quickly spit it out, opened a charcoal cap from her purse and emptied the contents in her mouth.

Okay, from now on, I have to eat my own food, she thought.

She dug into her pack to get some crackers, cheese sticks, and another can of tuna.

But first, she would finish eating the apple tart while looking closely for the stranger at the storage facility.

Graemes and Ortegan left at 9:00 and Marcia closed the front gate at 10:00 and went home.

Tomorrow would be Wednesday, and she would meet Richie for lunch.

In the morning however, she would go to the circuit court and start searching for names like Graemes, Ortegan, and Rossier. Maybe there would also be some information on Mr. Whitten.

She arrived home and the markers were in place at the apartment door. She entered the apartment and took a frozen pizza out of the freezer and ate in peace.

She was tired, and after bracing the door with a jamb pole under the knob, she went and showered and went to bed. Nothing would wake her tonight.

God was her refuge and strength.

30.

"She's got to go," Brahaim said to the Premiere who had just arrived for work.

"What did she do?"

"Taking pictures, found the water access door to the warehouse, I.D.'s the dealers driving in and out and takes more pictures, and even takes pictures of tire tread marks on the dirt."

"Guy across the street not able to shut her down?" the Premiere asked.

"She's blocking the energy somehow that comes from the storage facility. He's tried several times to stop her but she puts something in that booth window," Brahaim said.

"Okay, okay. The shipment's been made and getting cut so after tonight there'll be nothing there. Dealers will take it to 13th Street for mailing and distribution. So let her do what she wants. I think we're okay, and if not, call in Striden from the Highway Patrol to pass by a couple of times to give her a scare. Give him a call anyway: he's on the payroll."

"Alright," responded Brahaim.

"Skooly says don't worry. The system takes over at some time and shuts a person down electronically. Besides, it's no trouble to shut down that operation and go somewhere new. The drug trafficking will take care of itself after tomorrow when Graemes and Ortegan make their deliveries."

"Skooly. What do you know of him?" Brahaim asked.

"He's been around a long time, been groomed for this. He's a legal expert, got forty years experience in all the courts, knows a lot of people in high places, and he's very intelligent. He gets the right judge to push his agenda through."

"Okay. She's gone to bed. Muestro is still harassing her. Rossier has come and gone. And Miss Nozy here is lunching with her man tomorrow. All the other stations are clear, with the military conducting exercises over main threats. I'm leaving," said Brahaim."

It could be overwhelming at times for Premiere but his year's duty at this station would be up soon and he could walk away. It was simply an initiation period a new member of the organization had to suffer before obtaining a better position. First a member stalked someone, then covertly shuffled the victim's personal goods, used drugs on the victim, and then participated in applying remote sensing technology towards the victim.

The Premiere had been raised in this organization and was one step away from being financially secure the rest of his life. He could give the orders from a remote location without having to participate in the lawlessness of it all.

He walked up and down the floor looking for any red flags or alarms from the other cells.

And then he called Dominert in Switzerland.

"Hello," Dom answered.

"My friend, how is the weather there?"

"The snow is melting in the valley, the wine is good, and the cigars are smooth. Come on over."

"Shortly. Shortly. One matter to take care of and I'll be there."

"Can we help Johnnie?"

"No. No. Just called to reserve my room at the lodge."

"Plenty of room for registered guests."

And Dom terminated the call.

31.

Marcia woke only once, when she heard a dog yelping in an adjacent neighborhood. She had rolled back over and slept to 9:00 a.m.

Nice to know I haven't had any of that drug crap, she thought.

Today she would dress nice to visit the court and lunch with Richie. She would take and change into her work clothes in the booth at the warehouse with no problem since there would be no one around. The gun Rufus let her borrow was a problem; so she'd leave it in the car.

She looked outside to see a clear day with scattered clouds which usually meant showers in the late afternoon.

She put on a white short sleeve knit blouse with an open collar, khaki shorts, and leather sandals. Her blond hair was wavy and drifted on the top of her shoulders. An oval jade stone set in beaded antique 24K gold on a necklace accentuated her looks along with a smaller jade stone on her finger. Marcia hardly wore make-up other than plain lip gloss and sand colored nail polish. Her skin was olive colored, probably from the natural oils in her diet.

She had friends in the courthouse and she wanted to look good.

She made a cup of tea and sat thinking about the last couple of days. There hadn't been much stalking or energy attacks, but maybe that was because she was doing what the perpetrators wanted: simply checking three men in and out of the gate.

So I'm being used, she thought. And that just made her madder about this whole affair. And she knew that if she got closer to the truth – there would be pressure – and she could expect that soon after she visited the courthouse.

She put her tea cup on the kitchen counter and gathered her belongings for the night shift at the booth. She got the markers for the door, locked the door, and pulled it shut with the markers situated in different places.

She had made a Keep Out sign at the booth, and she took some tape out of her purse and taped the sign to the door. *Might do good to tell some of these people where to go,* she thought.

She stopped at the end of the sidewalk and opened her purse to find a business card for Captain Tellis of the police department in Newport News.

151

She would need that telephone number later. She got in her car and drove straight to the Courthouse. She parked in the lot and went to the clerk of the court's office; she had been there many times, dropping off hard copies of transcripts for the District Attorney and occasionally for a judge.

She walked in the office and saw Rita Naltonia first. Rita asked how she was doing.

"Got me a new job doing security work," Marcia answered with a smile.

"Girl, you go! Gets you out of the office some. How come you quit?" Rita said as she was shuffling papers.

"It was time for a change, and I like being outdoors," Marcia quietly whispered, "and I don't have to deal with a lot of you know who's around."

Rita nodded.

"Can you look up something for me?" Marcia continued.

"Like what?" Rita answered.

"A couple of fellows working at the warehouse I'm guarding."

"Well, if you got suspicions about criminal activity, their records would be over at the criminal court."

"Oh, I hadn't thought of that," Marcia said.

Rita said, "I can still find them from here though. What are their names?"

"Graemes, Ortegan, and Rossier," said Marcia.

"Ought to be easy enough," Rita said.

Marcia looked around the room while Rita was searching the names of criminal court cases and saw greenery plants were still on the window sills, seven rows of steel filing shelves were behind the clerks' desks, and there were burgundy colored cushioned chairs along the wall at the entrance door. A cash register sat on a lower portion of the clerk's front counter.

Rita motioned for her to come over. "Nothing on Rossier, but Graemes and Ortegan have first time charges for possession of illegal drugs."

Marcia asked, "What kind of drugs?"

"It doesn't say, but the cases were dismissed."

"Who was the counsel of record?" Marcia asked.

"Jerry Brandwell for the State, McListern for the defendants."

"McListern? Isn't that a partner in Jon Skooly's firm."

"Sure. Been representing drug defendants for years," Rita said.

"Rita, thank you so much for helping me."

"You're quite welcome, and I wish you luck in your new career. Hey, if you want a copy of these orders, criminal court has them."

"Okay, thanks." And Marcia walked out the door to the parking lot thinking she may have a breakthrough on the contents in the warehouse.

Sitting two rows back in the courthouse parking lot with a clear view of her car was Julian Muestro. *Apparently it wasn't enough to rummage her apartment and drug her foods,* he was thinking.

Maybe he could bribe some of his friends to scare her, or maybe he should call Skooly for a medical technician to implant her with a microchip.

But even with that, Muestro knew victims could disable them with high powered magnets – or destroy them with an electro-magnetic pulse. And the 60 coil winds put in victims for the electrical grid often disintegrated within years. Though most implants were biologically inert, scientists were able to distinguish synthetic substances. And he didn't want any part of that.

He would go home and think about it -- provide what pressure he could on her -- and that was it. If he went to jail, he went to jail, but he would make sure Skooly got his portion too.

Marcia got in her car and turned north on I-64 towards Williamsburg. Julian saw her turn and knew she was going to lunch with Richie from listening in on her phone conversations.

Jean's Deli was within walking distance of Richie's office, so she pulled into the parking area at his office and walked to the front door and opened it.

"Well hello stranger? Or should I say Stronger?" Margaret greeted her with a smile.

"Hey, Rufus is alright --gave me a job guarding an uninhabited warehouse. How are you?"

"Doing good, just getting ready to go out. And you?"

"Came here for lunch with the man. Is he available?"

"Will be. Be careful, he's been in court arguing motions this morning."

"Amazing how a man can be a bull sometimes?"

"And a child at other times," Margaret added. "He's all yours." And Margaret got up and left.

Marcia sat in a nearby chair and admired the office's colonial brick interior, the few pictures on the wall, and the visible iron rails covering the outside windows.

It felt like a prison except for the sun shining on the beige ceramic tile floor and the pine stained baseboard trim. Two cherry wood chair seats across from her had been covered with dark brown leather, and their leg bottoms mushroomed out forming animal paws of some kind.

She heard Richie talking on the phone, and then he put it down, shuffled some papers, and moved his chair back. He was on his way, and she promised herself to listen to his problems and be understanding of his morning's pre-trial motions.

The door opened and he smiled.

"You made it," he said, and he opened his arms to give a friendly hug. She kissed him on the cheek.

"I did. Couldn't wait to see you, and eat some good food."

"So how is the job?" he asked as he ushered her with one arm to the exterior door and opened it with the other.

"Fine," and she paused right there, not wanting to get into unfounded details. "Taking a gun class Saturday morning," she said looking at him.

"Wow, you're moving right along."

"Well, need to get on with this investigating work and protect myself."

Richie did not know what to say with that response, and for just a slight moment, his conscience bothered him, knowing he could be helping more.

155

There was little traffic as they crossed Adams Street — where workers were making an escape from the business district during lunch hour to go wherever.

Marcia felt comfortable for the first time in days now that she was with Richie. It seemed like it was always like that. Naomi was a good friend but Richie had this innate ability to lead, protect, and comfort her without saying a word. *I guess it's a man's way or something*, she thought. She certainly never had it at home with her father who was gone most of the time.

He opened the door for her and she stepped across the threshold into Jean's Deli. They sat at a table that was covered with a colonial times pictured tablecloth and had a host of condiments that had been set up on the far side.

The chairs were low-backed maple wood. The floor was a cheap linoleum tile, and two windows straddled the front door.

He sat down and took a deep breath.

"So what did you do this morning?" Marcia asked.

"Argued a few pre-trial motions for Bobby Braxtor. Argued for court jurisdiction, adverse litigant parties, and a jury if need be."

Marcia not wanting to stir things up but only to support him responded, "Well, I hope you win them all."

Richie looking at the sandwich menu said, "Hardly win them all, but if I win the first I can work on the others during trial."

"Like one step at a time," Marcia said.

"You got it. Now what would you like?"

"Hmmm . . . " Marcia uttered as she looked over a menu, "I'll have the Turkey and melted Swiss Cheese, Pickle, Spinach, Tomato, mayonnaise, oil, and vinegar on Black Rye bread – toasted."

"Sounds good. And I'll have Pastrami with Monterey Jack, on spinach flatbread with lettuce and tomato and the house dressing on the side. And shall we order some fries?"

"Yes, please."

A crowd started to filter in and a waitress hurriedly came over to the table with an order book in her hand, introduced herself, took the order, and brought back a pitcher of water, two paper cups, and two glasses of iced tea.

"So you work today?" Richie asked.

"I do. 2:00 at the warehouse with my six-shooter and a telephone. Oh, and a camera."

Richie laughed, and that's part of why he liked Marcia so much with her sense of humor, but also fearlessness.

"Hope you don't have to use either. And just what are you guarding anyway?"

"That's what I'm trying to find out. Three men come and go as they please. The only thing I've seen out of line is water was dripping from one of the vehicles as it left the gate."

"Could have been ice," Richie said.

"If it was clear water," Marcia responded.

Richie said no more thinking Marcia knew more about it than he did and probably already had figured out.

157

The food came on two large plates with coleslaw and a basket of fries.

Richie nodded at some acquaintances that walked by. Marcia was hungry and delicately put half the sandwich between her fingers and began to eat and talk at the same time.

"Always good sandwiches at Jean's," Marcia said. "How's the boy doing, Fredrico?"

"I haven't been back for a couple of days? Are you free this weekend?" Richie asked.

"Only after your golf game," Marcia said jokingly.

"Okay. Okay. You do have your way, don't you?"

"Sometimes," Marcia said.

Richie thought he could never win a conversation with her, yet in trial court he could pick apart the brain of a pathological liar or anyone testifying under oath about an incident. It intrigued him.

They talked about the weather, Naomi, Margaret, the latest construction projects on the highways, and a recent appointment of a judge. After forty-five minutes, they were finished and Richie left some cash in the tray for the waitress.

Richie said, "Well, let's get out of here. It was nice. I got work to do and you're going to Newport News."

"Okay. This was good. Thank you."

They walked to Marcia's car, where he gave her a kiss on the cheek and bid her goodbye.

Marcia drove straight to the warehouse and parked near the guard booth. She got the gun from the glove compartment, retrieved her backpack from the rear seat,

158

and went to the booth to change clothes to get ready for anything that may happen. She had a sense something would happen; she just didn't know what, but she would be ready.

No sooner than she had removed her clothes from the backpack she looked out of the corner of her eye to see a State Trooper's car parked on the dirt road leading to the compound. She thought it was a scare tactic because (1) the state had no jurisdiction on the city road here and (2) she hadn't done anything wrong.

She grabbed her camera, set it on automatic, and zoomed in on the car to try and get a picture of any numbers or the license plate.

She didn't do it discreetly; she walked outside the booth in her casual attire and tried to get a picture on the sunshine side of the car and looked for any item nearby that may be reflecting light to the car's side to lighten up the lettering since the sun was still overhead. Who knows, it may be a fake patrol car. She had been reading a photography book lately which gave her some insight on taking long-distance photos.

She took three pictures and went back into the booth to change clothes, while the patrol car slowly rode away.

She knew in her heart that wasn't the end of it, and sure enough, after Graemes and Ortegan arrived, three men walked near her booth looking at the compound's gate.

Discreetly, she closed the book she was reading and pulled the gun from the desk drawer. She opened the cylinder to check the load, closed it and waited, until they got within twenty yards.

They spread out a little. She didn't see any car around and she wasn't sure to what to do but to protect herself. So she stood up, with the phone ready to call 911 and the gun in her other hand.

Two men were unshaven, had shirt tails out, and wearing scuffed up blue jeans. The other man was clean shaven and dressed somewhat nice, so she figured he was in charge, and she looked him in the eye first.

"That's far enough," Marcia said trying to sound confident while showing them the gun and phone in her hands.

"Ah, well, we were just a little lost and looking for directions."

She pointed the gun near their way and they stopped walking towards her "Go look elsewhere. This area is restricted," Marcia said, and she held the gun a little higher.

"Maybe you don't understand what's going on," the well dressed man said.

"Understand perfectly. If you don't leave now, I'm calling the police if I don't shoot you first."

"Okay, okay, lady. But you better watch out for yourself," Mr. Pretty Man said.

"Got Mr. Ruger here for that. Now leave."

The man looked at his two friends and they walked slowly away talking to each other.

Marcia thought to herself, *you know, I'm beginning to like this investigative work and this gun thing has some power.* She waited until they turned the corner. *That's the end of that. Now to find out what's in the warehouse.*

She would ask Graemes on his way out tonight. If that answer wasn't satisfactory, she'd find a way to get in.

After the guys left, Marcia went into the booth to think about things. She was going to have to have help in her situation. She decided to call Rufus and tell him what happened.

She picked up the phone and called him and he answered quickly.

"Hey," knowing it was her.

"Had an incident here."

"What kind of incident?" Rufus asked.

"Thugs. Came up and tried to intimidate me. Said they were lost but they weren't. They were here to scare me."

"They still there?" Rufus asked.

"No. Ruger chased them away."

"Works every time. Speaking of Ruger, your firearms training class is at 9:00 at the firing range center in Poquoson. Can you make it?"

"Sure. I'm looking forward to it. This Ruger thing's got some power. Equalizes women and men."

"You're something. How's the occupants of the warehouse?"

"Everything seems normal except that guy Rossier who visited yesterday looked like a cat which just saw a boxer dog."

"Oh well, let's sit tight on it, draw some money, and discuss it Friday. Don't do anything dumb."

"But I was going to break in after they left to find out what's in there," Marcia.

"You'd be wasting your time. First, they wouldn't leave anything to be found, and second, they'd already know you're going to try."

"Well, just how is that Rufus since I've not told anyone but you?"

"Believe me. The establishment knows what a person is going to do before they do and are in fact instigating the event."

"The technology that advanced?" Marcia asked.

"Is," Rufus responded.

"But that's invasion of privacy."

"Undue coercion also, but that's the way it is. Hey, we'll talk later about it. Read a book or something and keep Mr. Ruger by you. Gets too bad, call me or Tellis."

"Oh, that reminds me. A trooper decided to stare at me from the corner when I first got to work."

"You're worth staring at."

"Rufus, you sure take a light hearted approach to all this uninvited invasion of my privacy."

"Part of the job honey. They get too close, give me a call."

"Okay, but I still want to look in the warehouse," Marcia responded.

"Women. Just don't get it sometimes," he said and sighed.

"I'll get it Friday," speaking of her paycheck. "See you at the office," and she smiled and ended the call.

Marcia was in no mood to read a book; she instead walked the fence perimeter looking at the warehouse wondering how she could get in, when she saw a loose piece of tin on the side of the building, as if someone had gotten in there before.

Graemes and Ortegan would be leaving late, so she made a plan to get in the next day before they came.

Meanwhile, she wanted to get to know this Captain Tellis, so she called the police and asked for him.

His secretary answered the phone, "Captain Tellis' office."

"Is the Captain in?" Marcia asked.

"And may I ask why you want to talk to him and who you are please?"

"I'm Marcia Lemay and work with Rufus Stronger. And Rufus said if I ever had any trouble to call the Captain."

"Have you had trouble?" the secretary asked.

"A little, like when three guys came up to me and tried to intimidate me."

"But there was no trouble?" The secretary responded.

"Could have been had not I pointed a gun at them and chased them away."

"Oh. Hold on."

"Captain Tellis here. Someone threaten you?"

"They told me I should watch out for myself."

"Shouldn't we all. How is Rufus?"

"Fine. Can you help me or not?"

"Sure, when someone does something wrong. We'll check it out."

"Okay. That's all I wanted to know. Thank you."

"You're welcome," and the Captain terminated the call.

Never hurts to spread the word a little Marcia thought, and she went back to reading her book.

32.

Marcia locked everything up at 10:00 and drove home satisfied she had performed her job well and confronted some thugs.

Guarding a warehouse was certainly easier than transcribing personal testimony all day and collating copies for lawyers, judges, and clerks.

She arrived home at 10:15. Everything on the door checked out, so she entered and sat down thinking about the day and how her faith was saving her. All those meetings she had attended at the Episcopal Church let her know there was a higher power in everyone's life if they just allowed it. But it took a deep humility and denial of self-thought before it could be attained. That was the hardest part, letting go of selfish desires and listening to a divine spirit. It took meditation and commitment, otherwise it would all be in vain. Morning, noon, and night she had said her prayers, and now she was realizing the benefits. She was not scared of anything.

Now that she had some job security, she thought about some personal desires – not selfish ones – but ones that would be joyful and fulfilling. She thought about Richie and whether he was ready for a life commitment, her apartment, nature, and exercise interests. The exercise would take care of itself now that she was on the street working. Once Richie got settled in his sole legal practice and became well respected among the judges, he may want her for life.

But the only thing she really wanted right now was a better place to stay, be out of the city congestion, and have a few good friends.

Reality suggested a different life with three thugs harassing her, someone breaking in her apartment and car, and a former boss who was obviously paranoid about her seeing forbidden files.

Thinking on these things only strengthened her faith in that divine power.

She was supposed to have lunch with Naomi this week.

Marcia retrieved a frozen Salisbury steak dinner from the freezer, micro-waved it for a couple of minutes, ate, showered, and went to bed. Tomorrow would be another day, and again, she thanked her divine power in advance for keeping her safe and happy.

166

33.

Marcia woke up to voices in her head telling her to quit her job, leave home, and have a drink of whiskey.

She tried to ignore them but nothing was working. She turned the radio on to drown them out but they were still there. She turned on a fan on to provide some white noise but they were still there, and then she tried singing out loud, but they were still there.

If that wasn't bad enough, there was a man working on his motorcycle with a noisy motor in back of her apartment and rumbling from the motor seemed to shake the building.

It was all designed to distract her.

Maybe she needed one of those magnets Naomi talked about to disturb whatever signal that was on her. Or maybe she should wear a hat with some foil in it to redirect the signals. And then she thought about an old article she had read where some man was sitting at an outside café in Italy and knew someone was trying to listen to his conversation; so he started jingling his silverware making a high frequency sound – and everything quieted.

Marcia banged a few pots together, and things did quiet somewhat. *There's got to be a way to shut this off,* she thought. *They probably know I'm going in that warehouse tonight to find out what's in there, so they're harassing me.*

Why is this happening to me? What is triggering this internal noise? Of course, they are trying to make me look mentally ill. But it won't work.

Marcia sat and continued to think: *the frozen food last night. The frozen food has preservatives and sometimes baking powder, and no telling what else. Okay, no more frozen food. I'll eat fruit and regular food and see if this noise goes away.*

So Marcia got an apple out of the refrigerator and sliced off two wedges and ate them, and sure enough, she began to feel better with the noise lessening.

She fixed a cup of tea, baked a potato and cautiously ate it. She began to quiet down and relax, said her prayers, and called Naomi.

"Hey girlfriend, how are things?" Naomi asked.

"Had a nice lunch with handsome yesterday. Went to Jean's."

"Alright . . . and how's he doing?"

"Fine. It seems like he never changes."

"Man's on a mission and a good one at that, working away from some of those people south. What's on your mind? I can tell something's going on."

"Woke up to those idiots talking to me this morning."

"Oh, Lord, Don't worry. It's just a computer program."

"A computer program?"

"That what it is, dictated to events in a person's life to defame, destroy, and seize."

"My God. This is serious."

"Yeah. Tell the leaders in the north country and you get a look of disbelief."

"Well, something's got to be done."

"How's investigating going?"

"Found the warehouse visitors to be convicted drug dealers that Brad what's his name represented."

"That's Skooly's thug. Makes deals with clients to help the firm."

"You know about that?"

"Pretty obvious the way they harass people just to stay out of jail."

"So all I got to do is start checking Skooly's former clients to find my stalker."

"Sounds like a start. Sounds like you may have two already!"

"But who do you call for help?"

"God Almighty is the best thing, after dealing with this no-win situation for ten years," Naomi said.

"Hey, you want to get together for Friday lunch?"

"Let's do next week honey. You and handsome have a great weekend and keep me posted," Naomi finished.

"Thanks for the tips Naomi."

"You're welcome. Watch your food, be safe, and don't let them poison your salt. That's their favorite."

"Wow. Okay, Thanks again," and Marcia laid the phone down in its cradle and sat thinking about what Naomi said.

Then she showered, dressed for work, and made plans to get in that warehouse before the guys showed up.

Marcia got to work a little early, parked her car in front of the booth and got out to open the booth's door. She put her belongings on the table – but the gun, flashlight, a screwdriver, cell phone, and a camera she put in a separate nylon bag and slung it over her shoulder.

She stepped out of the booth and locked the door. She opened the gate to the compound and closed it and locked it – the padlock was accessible from inside the gate.

She walked to the gravel filled area to the left side of the building and around the corner to see large rocks in the 5' area between the building and fence.

She walked carefully over the moldy rocks bracing her self against the building to stay balanced. Spider webs were numerous on the fence, and there were small hermit crabs scattered on the rocks. After about thirty feet, she reached the tin panel that was partially open.

She put her foot inside the bottom portion to pry open the middle portion. After she popped three metal fasteners, she slid between two wood studs and found herself on a concrete floor in the warehouse. *Not so difficult,* she thought as she brushed the dirt from her bottom pants legs.

The warehouse indeed looked like it had been a truck repair shop with grease stains on the floor, but she knew something else was going on here, and she began to look behind tarps, oil drums, and old tires.

She examined the back door exit to the river, the floor, and a nearby table she figured the men had been using for whatever. She saw a deck of cards on top of a cardboard box of old shop cloths, and off to the side, a box of plastic bags of several sizes. The floor there was oil stained, and most of the walls had some kind of grease stain, and that was it; there was nothing to show there were any drugs in the warehouse, as she kept looking behind items. The only new boxes she saw were all labeled All-Dri Cleaning Mix.

After thirty minutes of wandering around and taking a few pictures, she went back to the metal panel and slipped outside. She hand pounded the fasteners back in place with a screwdriver. She deftly walked back over the rocks to the front gate of the compound and unlocked it, opened it, and locked it back. She went to the booth, exhausted.

Graemes and Ortegan would be there shortly and she would act normal and wave them through the gate.

Something had happened a few days ago at the first of the month at that back door – she just hadn't figured it out.

She sat down to catch her breath and think about things. She took a canned drink and pack of crackers from her backpack and looked at her nylon bag. It was in the same place as she had left it, because she was marking everything and saw the straps lying in the same position on top of the bag.

When Graemes and Ortegan drove up and smiled, Marcia got up and unlocked the gate and waved them through. And she locked the gate back.

She went back to the booth and decided to look at the eight pictures she had taken, looking for any clue that would help her figure out the operation.

When she got to the picture of the plastic bags, she stopped, knowing they were being used currently because the outside boxes were clean.

And then she thought about drugs. It was a drug transition point, where a boat delivered them either at the first of the week or month and Graemes and Ortegan were repackaging the delivery load. *But how would the drugs get on the boat?*

But at least now she knew what was happening and she was being used to guard the operation by big perpetrators somehow. They would surely get rid of her shortly.

And that's what happened when Rufus called at 5:00 to let her know their contract at the warehouse was terminated as of Friday at 10:00 p.m.

"No problem," he said. "You can help me, and there's plenty of work. Mr. Hendricks still wants his wife watched on occasion and there's this job I'm doing checking out delivery trucks."

"Okay," she had said. Sitting at the guard booth was getting kind of boring but she wouldn't give up her knowledge about the operation. She'd call Tellis and tell him her suspicions about when the next delivery of drugs would be made.

"Come by and get your money tomorrow. I'll return the keys Monday," Rufus had said. "Don't forget your firearms class Saturday, and once you qualify, file a form with the court to get a permit to carry a concealed weapon."

Marcia thought about these happenings – how someone was in control of the warehouse and her. But she could have an impact on stopping the drug flow if she played it cool and waited until the right time to report it. What she wanted to know was whether the delivery was on Monday or at the first of the month. That much she could find out later.

Marcia looked again at the pictures and the All-Dri packs, which seemed to stand out from among the other items: the labels were new looking.

Maybe that was the drug's disguise, she thought.

Well, it was over for her now. There'd be another project.

The rest of the evening was uneventful and Marcia left the booth to go home at 10:00, with one more day to work. But first, she'd see Rufus at noon to get her new assignment and money.

"Well, that takes care of her at that job. Now if she'll just be quiet," the Premiere said to Brahaim in the bunker.

"Well, she won't be quiet. Women are not quiet Johnny. They talk and talk and talk. Give them a subject – and they know everything about it – or want to know everything about it."

"Eh, they are curious, but what's life without women. They calm the nerves, make joy in the middle of stress, and they soothe the tired muscles," the Premiere responded.

"And they put men in jail," Brahaim said.

"Men that violate maternal heritage. Well, certainly. But without women, there would be no life."

"Always wondered about that Johnny. Woman comes from man but woman gives birth to man. A big circle."

"This one has some spunk, and unless we take action, Skooly and the whole arena could come crashing down."

"Skooly's an old man with lots of friends. Who knows? Maybe it's time for him to bow out," the Premiere finished.

The Premiere walked over to a monitor that showed Graemes and Ortegan finishing repackaging heroin into three sizes of plastic bags which would be distributed at stops along the I-95 corridor to Washington D.C. The men would leave Friday evening, deliver a few bricks, and continue to distribute packages through the weekend when police patrols were minimal and vehicular traffic was lighter. The money due the organization was due the 10th day of each month in multiple payments under $10,000 to escape financial detection alarms. It would be sent by courier or mailed by cashier's check. Cashier's checks were usually cashed at one of two locations: Finchech Savings and Loans in Hampton or Annandale, Virginia.

"There are newcomers on the island," Johnny said with a stern face.

"I've noticed, maybe a few but probably tourists, or relatives of the folk there," Brahaim responded.

"Maybe, but let's have our people keep an eye on them just in case."

"Okay. I'll tell Lieutenant Geraldo when I get to the barracks," said Brahaim. "You're not getting paranoid, are you?"

"I think you're the one getting paranoid. Just do as I say," Johnny finished, and he walked away to sit at a desk to write a letter to his wife back home.

34.

Marcia awoke Friday morning to a rainy day.

She fixed herself some decaffeinated coffee, oatmeal with butter and honey, and had one can of evaporated milk.

She felt God's presence -- a divine intervention of peace. Everything slowed around her as if a weight had been lifted off her shoulder. It was the same feeling when she was younger and lonely -- when her mom was unsociable.

Maybe it was time again to start reading the scriptures and go to church, she thought. She needed reassurance she was on the right path in life.

But then she thought about Richie. *Was he taking me away from my closeness to God?*

How safe and needed she felt with him.

And she wanted to see him. She didn't know where this relationship was going because of her problems though.

Hopefully it will work out.

She went to open a closet door only to find it was drooping slightly and rubbing against the door jamb.

Maybe it's just a coincidence the top hinge screw is loose, she thought as she inspected to door's two hinges. *Or maybe it's not.*

There were other oddities happening she didn't understand; trash underneath the bag in the kitchen garbage container, dirty clothes in the clean clothes area, and a pair of slacks that reappeared after missing for months.

Now she understood completely, and she vowed revenge.

The toilet flapper chain had been shortened to make the water run continually, something toxic was in her shampoo, some can food had been missing then returned (she discarded the cans), a space rug had some kind of strange dust on it, and a light bulb flickered off and on from the ceiling in the hallway.

Naomi had warned her about such things, so it wasn't a surprise to find the loose door hinge.

She'd get through this like she did when she was young and crazy things happened. At least by knowing Christ, she knew it wasn't her! It was the devil!

It was life as usual, and if the perpetrators were trying to drive her crazy, they were wasting their time.

She washed dishes, took a shower, and dressed in work clothes to visit Rufus and go to the warehouse booth.

Maybe tomorrow night she would see Richie but first she would go to the firearms class in the morning to get qualified for a gun permit.

She arrived at the rear entrance to Rufus' office at 12:00 and walked around the old building to the front door entrance and up the stairs to the interior door.

She knocked once lightly and Rufus answered, "Come in."

"Hi Rufus. I'm so glad to see you."

"And you too. Why you so happy today?"

"It's payday, right? That's what we agreed on," Marcia said.

"Oh yeah," and he reached in his drawer and gave her an envelope with a check. "And the gun please."

Marcia reached in her purse and gave him his gun. "But will I need one for tomorrow?"

"They have some. Why don't you try a few out in the shooting gallery and see which one you like. They have pink guns, revolvers, magazine loaded guns, and all kinds. But I suggest something light weight, easy to use but with a safety trigger, and a short barrel. For any long distance shooting, call me and I'll bring a rifle." Rufus smiled.

"Thanks Rufus?" Marcia said with a grim look.

"Now bring me up to date on the warehouse."

"Not much to update other than plastic bags, All-Dri sand, and lots of grease on the walls."

"And just how do you know all this?" Rufus inquired.

"Well . . . there was an opening in the wall and I went in and checked it out."

"Plastic bags? Sounds like drug dividing to me," Rufus responded.

"Yeah, and maybe the water from the truck was from a batch a boat brought in, but I never heard or saw a boat."

"Don't mean there wasn't one," Rufus said.

"What do you mean?"

"You could have been distracted, the boat could have drifted in or maybe what you saw wasn't there or something was there that didn't look like it when it was there."

"You know about that stuff?"

"Certainly. I'm an investigator. Just take pictures when you *don't feel* you need to."

"Did at the warehouse," Marcia smiled.

"Let me see them," Rufus said anxiously.

Marcia got the camera from her purse and turned it on. Displayed were pictures of items in the warehouse; she showed them to Rufus one at a time.

"Well, not a lot of evidence for drug usage but it's a start. Circumstantial anyway," Rufus said. "Make hard copies of them and put them in the safe over there," pointing towards the key box. "You never know when things like those may come in handy."

"Call Tellis?" Rufus asked.

"Did. Gave a hello and told him my suspicions," Marcia responded.

"Okay. Got something else for you. You remember the Hendricks lady, right?"

"Yeah. The heavy set blonde at the deposition hearing trying to steal from her old man."

"Well, the mister wants to know where she's at, who's she with, etc . . . . Can you handle this?"

"Sure, but I'll have to change my make-up so she doesn't recognize me."

"Don't change too much. You're pretty as you are."

Marcia blushed a bit and rolled her eyes. She looked towards the window briefly when several pigeons lifted off a building roof across the street and flew eastward toward the bay.

"Okay? Get to know her. Find out what she's doing. She'll be at Sandler's Country Club on hot afternoons at the pool. Keep track of your hours and turn them in Friday. Try not to be obvious or over friendly."

"Primarily what are we looking for?"

"Fraud. Like where's she getting her money from, bad checks, insurance policies, or maybe she's prostituting. Just whatever," and Rufus reached in his desk and brought out a recorder and showed it to Marcia. "Just keep it in your little purse with your make-up. It's voice activated so you don't have to worry about turning it on."

:"And just how do I do that with a bathing suit on?"

"It's only 2" square."

"Oh. Well there is that."

"Great. Check back with me around Thursday," Rufus said.

Marcia got up from her chair and said, "Thanks Rufus. Any tips on the firearms class?"

"Do not wave the gun at the instructor and for God's sake load the gun correctly to feed the chamber, not the barrel."

Marcia smiled and said, "Okay, I'll tell them you showed me."

Rufus shook his head and said, "Have a great night and weekend. Drop back by here and put the gate key in the box."

"I don't have a key to the office," Marcia said.

Rufus walked over to the key box and retrieved an office key and gave it to her.

"Any questions?"

"Yeah, you got a holster for this gun I'm getting? Your gun rubbed against my side terrible."

"No. Wait until you get qualified. If you don't blow the instructor's foot off, we'll get you one."

"Sordid Rufus. See you next week," Marcia said as she exited the door and descended the steps and went to her car money in hand with a free weekend after work.

If it rains next week, she could be off work for a couple more days if Ms. Hendricks doesn't show at pool side.

Marcia drove to the warehouse and entered the booth. She felt peace and knew it was because the perpetrators had stopped targeting her so bad, probably because they had gotten what they wanted with a drug operation, but she'd figure it out.

That's alright, she thought, *I will find out when the next drug shipment is arriving and report it. My God, there are enough drug deaths in this area.*

The night was uneventful as Richie didn't call and there were no newcomers to the gate area, no strange police, and no activity at the mystery self-storage facility.

But that didn't mean someone had stopped the pressure on her, especially at home.

She looked forward to attending gun training class in the morning and checking the river for any boats that came along at the warehouse dock at sunset Monday, technology or no technology.

She locked up the booth door at 10:00 and drove to Stronger's office and walked up the stairs to open the door and put the keys from the warehouse in the lock box. She laid the job's journal on Rufus's desk and exited the building and went homeward. She did not see anyone following her.

She parked her car and went inside her apartment after checking the markers at the jamb.

She was relieved she had completed a week of work.

She was excited and sat down on the couch to some soothing music by Loreena McKennitt on a disc player.

Then she went to the kitchen and opened a can of chicken breast meat and steamed some rice. She came back to the couch to eat and felt more peace.

The next morning Marcia was up at 7:00 and ate some oatmeal that tasted okay. She dressed in a casual smock top and loose fitting pants which would enable her to be comfortable holding and shooting a gun. She put on tennis shoes that had no hard edges so she could maneuver easily. She arrived in Poquoson at 9:00 and found the building for the gun class.

There were ten other people there: some looked like hunters, some looked like regular citizens, and there were some law enforcement personnel.

There were four different classes: firearms laws, ethics and firearms, a gun safety class, and options to carry a firearm publicly.

After lunch, there was a pre-shooting session where everyone practiced stances to shoot a firearm, and finally a shooting exercise –firing at a target thirty yards three times – to get a qualifying certificate to present to a court and get a permit to carry a firearm.

Marcia did surprisingly well at the live fire exercise after remembering Rufus' tip about aiming a little low and left at the center mark. She did find pulling the trigger lifted the barrel up and to the right slightly – so she adjusted and came within a few inches of hitting the center mark on the target. And now she was used to the kickback and noise of the gun. They let her use a .38 caliber pistol also.

The instructors quickly gave out the achievement certificates to all the attendees and Marcia gleefully left the range and classroom area eager to tell Richie what she had accomplished.

Marcia was driving home about 3:00 but remembered Richie was probably playing golf since it was a sunny day. She would call him later.

She stopped off at a mall on the way home and bought a new bathing suit for the country club meeting with Ms. Hendricks next week. She also bought a few other items knowing the perpetrators had probably spoiled some clothing at home.

The perpetrators often tore underwear, put holes in socks, or stained new linens. It was insane what they did.

After picking up a container of noodles and vegetables at a Chinese restaurant, she arrived home at 5:00. She put her dinner on the counter and quickly put away her new clothes and sat down to call Richie. She wasn't going anywhere tonight -- it had already been a long day.

She called and he was home.

"Well, how did it go?" he asked.

"Just great. I got qualified with two shots a few inches from the man's face."

"What man's face?" he asked.

"The one on the target the instructors had set up. The target had different colors on it, with the top half of a man's torso. I went for the face."

"Thought you were supposed to shoot in the chest."

"I like to stop them from talking first, and if they can't see me, they can't shoot back," said Marcia.

"Hadn't thought about that," Richie said.

"Seen that on the cowboy movies too, and always try to have the sun at your back so they can't see you."

"Jeez, you got this down pat."

"Hey, I'm an investigator and need to get it right. How was golf?"

"Average. Shot an 88 and won $5.00 with two birdies."

"But how much does it cost to play?" she asked.

"We won't talk about that."

"Sounds counter productive," Marcia.

"You counter productive?" Richie asked.

"No. I produce. Where's your memory?"

"Probably needs to be joggled," Richie said.

"I can do that," Marcia.

"I know," Richie said.

Marcia and Richie agreed to get together the next week. Besides, she had to conduct strategy for seeing Starr Hendricks, and she wanted to try on her new bathing suit.

35.

On Sunday morning Marcia felt good until she looked out the window and saw a sky full of smog and planes flying over.

Naomi had warned her about the military spraying chemicals in the sky to facilitate transmissions of subliminal messaging, and now she believed it, with a song hitting her head.

She sat with her robe on in the living room and thought about the Lord's Day and how good it would be to go to the old Episcopal Church -- but it was too far to drive this morning.

There was one nearby in Hampton, and she needed that hope again that she found around other believers and Christ in a church.

In the midst of indecision about worldly ventures, she certainly did not need to try and figure out things herself and end up in trouble or dead.

She decided to put her worries in the arms of God. Today, she would worship somewhere in peace -- which was enough to get her up and get dressed for church.

Sure someone might come in her apartment while she was gone, but she could not live in fear the rest of her life: she would figure out if someone had come in.

She washed, put on a black skirt, short sleeve white blouse and tan cotton buttoned sweater. Her shoes were black leather with two inch heels.

She washed the exterior of her purse slightly because carrying it around the work area had gotten dust on it from the nearby dirt road.

She combed her hair and walked back through the apartment and tried to get a visual look of where everything was placed in case someone came in.

She grabbed her Bible from a shelf under the coffee table and grabbed a few markers for the door.

For added security, she dropped the broom handle behind the door just before closing it so if anyone opened the door, the handle would be moved outward.

It was 10:30 and she'd be at church for an 11:00 service.

The streets were empty for the most part. Most people stayed home on Sundays.

She got to the church in 25 minutes and parked the car in an empty space. She walked briskly to the front door and opened it and was greeted by an older well dressed

187

man who offered her a program while music from an organ played an introductory slow melody that invited meditation and prayer.

There were some 40 people already seated in a church that could seat 75, with eight rows of twelve foot pews on each side of the aisle.

Candle holders were on small tables on both sides of the speaker's podium, and a table of flowers fronted the altar.

Tall vertical stained glass windows of the apostles surrounded the room, and a red carpet adorned the choir stage area and the elder's platform.

A white nylon drape covered the podium with an emblem of Jesus as King of Kings.

She sat down and quietly reflected on her situation and God's omnipresence. She gave thanks for her new job, Richie, and a place to live. There were trials and troubles in all aspects of life – but she felt they would pass away.

She sang some hymns with the congregation and gave a monetary offering when a plate was passed around from row to row.

She listened to the preacher's message of performing good works in life without selfish expectations – but to rely solely on God's provisions and supplies.

It reminded her of a message from Jesus about following and working for righteousness – and how provisions would be given as needed.

She left the church satisfied yet felt a yearning to stay there and become involved in weekly activities but she knew it wouldn't work right now because of the targeting and her situation.

The perpetrators would find a way to shame her and turn people against her: they may even be in the church. Part of the program, Naomi said, is to defame a person and make a person look bad.

She decided to get some take-out food from a Chinese restaurant and eat at home. So far, there hadn't been a problem at the Chinese restaurant, but she knew the workers there too could be bribed into tainting a person's food, if they had advance notice and recognized the victim.

She found and put her sunglasses on, retrieved a black scarf from the back seat and put it around her neck, and walked into the restaurant to order.

She'd call Richie later, if he hadn't called her. It was Sunday, and she wanted to do nothing.

36.

Marcia began to develop a strategy for getting to know Starr Hendricks, the estranged wife of Mr. Hendricks, who had been sued for all that he was worth, including personal assets he derived before the marriage. If he would have just kept better records of the dates of his acquisitions, he wouldn't have had this problem. Of course, there wouldn't be any problem at all had he not married the blundering woman.

Marcia was unsure of whether to present herself just as she is -- or disguise herself as another woman – in front of the Hendricks woman.

No. Ms. Starr isn't stupid. She's surely to figure that out. I'll just be honest with her – tell her I'm in between jobs.

Monday morning Marcia took her certificate from the firearms training class to court and filled out a form to get a permit to carry a gun. A background check would have to be conducted by the state and it would take a couple of weeks to process the form, she was told.

After leaving the courthouse, she stopped by the library to return a book and get a couple more books, along with browsing the newest titles. The library back in Va. Beach had been a sanctuary at times – it would be quiet there and she could also find reading material for her brothers. The Newport News library was just as peaceful with its isolated presence away from the town district at the end of a small community of well built homes.

After leaving the library, she went home to take a nap and think more about the warehouse and what was going on there. Normally, she didn't have to take time out to think about something: it just came naturally. But with a constant noise in the air surrounding her, someone was purposely disturbing her with something.

Marcia wanted to know whether a boat could dock at the river side of the warehouse and somehow unload something.

It would surely dock after sunset, she thought, *so as not to be visibly seen by someone. Graemes and Ortegan would still have time to load up whatever it was they were distributing.*

She would drive down to that perch out at the water's edge to see if a boat flanked the warehouse this evening.

At 6:00, she rode over to the perch and parked the car. There was a person in the warehouse booth, just as Rufus speculated about the renter changing guards every week.

A few gulls flew by, pleasure and business boats were on the water, and traffic over the bridge tunnel began to shine with vehicle lights reflecting off the guard rails and the humid air. The sun began to set over the horizon illuminating clouds from underneath. And finally, it was dark; there was no sign of any boat. She waited thirty more minutes but all was calm.

Then she began trying to fit the Rossier fellow into the puzzle. *What was he really doing at the warehouse? And maybe he was the boater?*

She started up the car's engine and went home satisfied deliveries were being made to the warehouse once a month. She would tell Captain Tellis later about her suspicions.

Tuesday started out as a slightly humid day but the sun was shining and Marcia thought it would a good day indeed to go to the pool and see if Starr was there.

She would be a first time guest and able to enjoy the club amenities for two visits without a paying a membership fee, thanks to Rufus, who seemed to know everyone in town and how to get his way into any facility.

She already had packed her bags for the affair, with her swimsuit, shades, book, lotion, and secret recorder, which fit nicely in her padded swim suit top. . .

How nice it is to be on my own schedule! She thought as she drove to the country club.

She arrived there shortly before noon and checked in at the pool's entrance – said she had been invited by Rufus Stronger.

After showing the attendant her driver's license and signing a non-liability form, Marcia found the women's locker room and changed into her new one piece soft blue bathing suit and packed her bag with her regular clothing and grabbed a towel off a gurney and walked along the pool's perimeter to find a lounge chair that would give her a good look at anyone entering the pool area.

She put her goods on a nearby wooden table and sat down in an adjoining chair. She took her book out of the carrying bag and sat back and relaxed.

She looked pretty good for having been sitting in an office several years and wasting away typing transcripts. Her legs were slightly tanned from being outdoors and feeding ducks at a pond in the evenings and weekends. Her hair was thick and wavy -- probably from all the oatmeal she ate. Her breasts were smooth and rounded and fit comfortably in her bathing suit even with the tiny recorder placed in the middle that she had tried on earlier.

Her thin arms and shoulders had been toned from the massages she would get at a natural health center in Williamsburg once a month from an older woman who was the fittest old person Marcia had ever seen.

Before she got too cozy, she picked up a piece of scrap paper off the concrete to throw away and walked the perimeter of the pool area looking for a garbage can so she'd understand the area. She also wanted to know if anyone was in the parking lot outside the see-through perimeter fence looking at her.

The ceramic floor tiles around the pool area were slippery, as Marcia almost slipped near the pool's edge as she was walking. Or was it done remotely?

There was one main diving board. And the pool had a shallow end that swelled to six feet with a drop ladder on each side.

Good to know this stuff. I mean who knows; someone might try to kill the woman or me! Marcia was thinking.

Recently she had all kinds of thoughts running through her head being an investigator. Friends would say she was paranoid -- Marcia thought she was smart – paranoid being safe.

Marcia found a garbage can and went to a lounge chair near her goods and straightened out a towel to its length. She laid down with her head resting so she could see the pool entrance.

Of course she knew her perpetrators would love this, as they were probably taking pictures and videos of her and selling them. But what could she do about it? This was her normal life of having grown up near the beach sun bathing and swimming; she would not deviate from what she knew was healthy and happy.

Twenty minutes later, Starr Hendricks showed up under a large blue floppy plastic straw hat that was wavering in the wind. She was toting a bulky bag that looked to be loaded with a week's provisions.

37.

Could be living in her car I suppose. Came here to get cleaned up, Marcia was thinking as she saw Starr enter the pool area.

Starr found a lounge chair on the other side of the pool and set the bag on a nearby chair with one hand while holding a drink with the other.

Pleasure always exceeds function with Starr, Marcia thought.

The drink looked like a Daiquiri with a slight green color in a clear glass with s slice of lemon wedged at the top of the rim. Marcia had immediately taken a picture with a mini-camera and zoomed in for a better look.

Starr brushed some of the dust off the lounge chair with a whisk of her free hand and sat down.

She took off her sheer top exposing her busty figure and one piece red bathing suit. It actually contrasted nicely with her strawberry blonde hair, Marcia thought.

Starr sat back and slowly sipped her drink while looking around the pool.

After Starr relaxed, Marcia decided to wait a few minutes and go swimming near Starr's side of the pool.

Marcia removed the recorder from her suit and deftly walked to the ladder and entered the cool water to reach out and side stroke her way the length of the pool and back.

With all the ocean water and pools surrounding Marcia's childhood home, she had learned to swim at an early age at a leisurely pace – stroking after exhaling, and inhaling after feeling her airless body drop -- gradually floating back to the top of the water maintaining a rhythm with normal breathing.

A person could swim all day when the breathing equaled the flotation and rhythm of the body movement.

On occasion she would float on her back, and when she felt herself dropping, she would take a backward stroke to regain her buoyancy.

After twenty minutes, she went to the ladder climb on Starr's side of the pool and rested before exiting the pool

Marcia climbed the pool ladder and walked slowly to Starr's area still dripping wet and looking for a stray towel.

Marcia wouldn't have to start a conversation with Starr – she was confident Starr would begin talking considering her rhetoric at a deposition hearing, and now she was drinking loose lipped alcohol.

And that's what happened. While Marcia was shaking the water from her tanned thin legs, Starr spoke up, "Oh dear, you swim so well."

"Love to swim, every since I was a child," Marcia said while bending her head and wringing water from her hair. .

"And where was that?" Starr replied.

"Next door at Virginia Beach."

"Haven't I seen you somewhere?" Starr asked.

"Maybe. Hold on and let me get another towel," Marcia said as she quickly retreated to her chair area and grabbed two towels – one with the recorder safely tucked inside it.

"Um. I'm not sure," Marcia said as she came back to Starr's seat. "Where do you work?"

"I work with my boyfriend now. He owns a lot of restaurants and stores," Starr said.

Starr looked at Marcia briefly and turned a straw in the drink.

"Oh. You're Mrs. Hendricks."

"Why yes. How do you know me?" Starr said.

"I was the stenographer that day of testimony when that stingy husband of yours was trying to rob you."

"That's the truth. That man has more money than the law allows and I helped him get some of it," Starr said.

"Men don't always appreciate our work."

"No, darling, nor our love. But I got one now and he's got plenty of money."

"He must be busy," Marcia responded.

"He's got plenty of help," Starr said as she proudly looked over at her bag.

Wind rippled a table umbrella canvas covering nearby while dust and leaves swirled up against the corner of the enclosed pool fence. Some leaves traveled the pool's walkway and finally settled along an uplifted edge. A few clouds appeared overhead.

"Well, there you go. Who needs Mr. Hendricks?" Marcia said.

"Got that right. He'll be done when I get my share."

Marcia decided she had learned enough about that issue and changed the subject. "I just love this pool. What can I do to join this club?" she asked.

"Know someone or pay the dues. They got great drinks at the country club bar," Starr said lifting her glass and curling her legs.

"Hey, it's nice chatting with you. Going over to read the latest thriller and get some sun," Marcia said.

"Anytime darling. Hey, what kind of work are you doing now?"

"I am looking for a job," Marcia responded as she started to walk away.

Starr said, "Well maybe the old man has one for you. Good luck."

Marcia thought, *Hmmm . . . maybe he does. But I shouldn't have said anything about a job. I'm still learning about this investigating business.*

38.

Rufus had asked Marcia to come to the office to work Wednesday and learn about some paperwork.

When she arrived, he showed her the billing process, rates per hour, contract agreements that shielded the business from liability, the computer programs, and financial information.

At first, Marcia didn't want anything to do with desk work again, but a small break from investigating would be okay, and she needed to know how to perform internet background checks and investigate family information on the firm's clients.

Rufus was allowing her to become a full fledged partner, and for that, she was thankful. She delved into the computer programs and forms that were most often used to for billing, journalizing, and time keeping.

But Marcia had a few other things on her mind also --
like finding out more about Graemes and Ortegan. She
would make sure Tellis had all the information needed for
an arrest when the next month's drug delivery took place.

"So tell me about Starr?" Rufus asked while Marcia
was on the computer searching and becoming familiar
with its software.

"Nice lady but definitely money minded," Marcia
responded.

"How so?" Rufus asked as he extracted a few files from
a nearby cabinet. "What's she doing?"

"Got her a rich boyfriend who owns retail stores."

"So let's get this straight. She's sued the Mister for
abuse and alimony but she couldn't get it because he
wasn't at fault. He wins the divorce and now they have to
split the assets of the marriage. She only gets half of what
they earned together in the marriage, and more than
likely he is claiming assets to be personal so she won't get
a dime --because from what I understand he started most
of his trucking business before they got married. So they
are fighting over equitable distribution and he wants to
know how much assets she has, especially if they are
hidden and personal," Rufus said.

"Sounds right. She couldn't get him on fault to pay
alimony and was trying to act like a poor person by not
working and receiving no income. That didn't work. Now
she's found a man who's got some money, just in case
she's not happy with equitable distribution from Mr.
Hendricks," Marcia responded.

"Mr. Hendricks is just protecting his butt. That's all this is about. And who knows, maybe the woman has been hiding assets on the side. But if there isn't no fraud or deceit, it just isn't there," Rufus said. "Ain't Richie involved in this somehow?" he asked.

"Used to be," Marcia said while typing her name in the computer as an employee of Stronger's Investigations. "He represented Mr. Hendricks in divorce proceedings but relinquished the equitable distribution phase to Bryan Salter – said accumulative assets over two million dollars was too much for him. Does Bryan know we're even doing this?"

"Mister H. asked me personally to do this, so I said 'okay'. Hey, at $100.00 hour it was hard to turn down."

"Good," Marcia said. "How do I get these reports printed?"

"Turn the printer off the fax mode. Still only got one telephone line here," Rufus said.

"Oh. Okay."

"What reports?"

"The warehouse workers' rap sheets, home addresses, and Rossier's pad in Va. Beach for a feather in our cap with Tellis. And who knows, there may be a reward."

"Or a grave. Be nice to have a feather in our cap. Good to stay in good relations with the cops. I need their help on matters like who's watching who, plus I don't want to overlap an investigation."

"Sure," Marcia responded.

"So, can we get an address on this boyfriend of Starr's? I need to give Mr. H. something. And can you find any other acquaintances Starr may have had during her marriage. That's what we really need."

"Hmmm.....might can find the address of the boyfriend, but I'll need to dig more into her past, next time."

"Okay, work on that, so we have something to give Mr. H. I mean. She may be driving one of Mr. Hendricks's cars and using it for something other than pleasure. Get the license number off that please," Rufus said.

"She may be using us," Marcia said as she browsed criminal records of the Peninsula counties.

"What'd you just say?" Rufus said.

"She may be using us, like the rest of this operation is," replied Marcia.

Rufus got up from his seat and went to the window to think. He was initially hired by Mr. Hendricks to get dirt on Starr, which he did. But it didn't make sense for him to continue to watch Starr. *Is she just a distraction?* Rufus wondered.

A delivery truck below stopped in the street while cars were backed up behind it waiting on oncoming traffic to clear. The driver was lifting the back paneled door open of the truck to retrieve several boxes and a dolly to carry them. Smoke from the exhaust of a pickup truck slowly wound its way up through the narrow adjoining buildings trying to find its way to escape over the roofs. And Rufus turned away.

But Marcia was right. Starr was a distraction from him finding out what was in the warehouse and Whitten's building, but what the perpetrators didn't figure on was Rufus hiring Marcia for help.

Marcia spoke up, "Wow, not only do these guys have rap sheets in this county but they got charges in Henrico County also."

"Tellis will like that. That should be enough," Rufus said. "Mail it off to him and put a note in there with your thoughts – and the pictures of the items in the warehouse."

"Alright boss. So what's next in this line of work?" Marcia asked. "I can't do Starr all the time."

"No, you can't. I want you to help me on this counterfeit goods case."

"Such as?" Marcia responded.

"The usual. Figuring out where they're coming from, where they're going, and who's in charge. Once we get the evidence, we'll turn it over to the State Attorney's office. Well, that's my plan anyhow, but somehow original plans never seem to turn out the way they were intended."

"So why aren't we breaking into the storeroom and getting a few packages?"

"Money dear. Whitten pays me to sit there to watch the proceedings, so I do," Rufus said.

"Kind of like the warehouse," Marcia responded.

"Uh huh. You think we're being used again?"

"Uh huh. No doubt," Marcia said. "But let's take their money and turn them in."

"Sounds like a plan, if we don't get turned in to the open sea in a wooden box. Work it a few weeks, turn it over to the feds, and go to the next job, if we're still alive," Rufus said sarcastically.

"Think our employer may terminate us before then?" Marcia asked.

"Maybe, unless we're dumb and don't anything too smart," Rufus responded.

"We can do that."

"Meet me here tomorrow morning at 5:00," Rufus asked.

"Kind of late, isn't it?" Marcia asked.

"5:00 in the morning. Early bird gets the worm."

"Bird gets donuts too?" Marcia asked.

"I'll bring the donuts. Just bring your sitting seat, because that's what we do — we sit and watch. It's the best part of the job," Rufus said.

"Okay Rufus. When and where do I use the bathroom?" Marcia asked.

Rufus rolled his eyes and looked out the window back across the street at the passing traffic and Rosie's Cafe, where there were always pretty girls dining for lunch.

39.

Marcia went home satisfied she was learning more about the intricacies of operating a business.

Rufus had all his expense and revenue accounts in the computer, and he had figured up a balance sheet of liabilities and assets for the past year. He said he spent at least thirty minutes a day on book work.

Marcia went to bed early and wasn't bothered by too much adverse energy other than a kind of light which would flash before her at times. *It must be radar*, she thought.

Before sleeping, she would put a black mask over her eyes as Naomi had suggested – who also said something about the perpetrators making drugs which bothered the optic nerve and made victims sensitive to light. Naomi said it facilitated remote neural targeting with subliminal scenes of the past. "There is no post traumatic stress illness," she said. "They take scenes of the past and send them back to individuals to make them think they are mentally ill. If a person is not able to concentrate on the issue at hand, it's because of the targeting system. But that certainly doesn't exclude a person from doing something wrong and not being held accountable for it. God knows."

Marcia thought Naomi had lost her mind talking about this stuff but now thought her to be the smartest woman on earth.

Marcia awoke to the alarm clock at 4:00 a.m. Thursday morning and hurriedly dressed in khaki shorts, a dark blue short sleeve collared pullover, and some sandals. There would be no running for her today, or walking over boulders.

She arrived at the office parking lot at 5:00 and waited for Rufus, who drove up in five minutes and opened the door for her. She stepped up into his Toyota and watched the town's activities as he drove to an empty parking space at 13th Ave. and Waters Street.

"We'll hang around here until after the sun rises anyway. A Ford transport van usually pulls in just before light and unloads some packages and picks up some. What we need is a license number of that vehicle and identification of the driver and helper," Rufus said as he handed Marcia a donut.

"So why don't I tip toe around the corner to get a better look at the action?" Marcia asked.

"One, because we don't want to take a chance on being identified, and two, we don't know who is looking at us."

"And just who is looking at us?" Marcia asked.

Rufus did not respond but sat silent, looking at a blinking street light, an "open" sign across the street on a book store door that was surely locked, and the foggy windows of a glass repair shop that had left its air conditioner on too long creating condensation.

"Ain't sure yet, like what you are experiencing," Rufus said.

"It's crazy when someone watches your every move and then tries to hurt and defame you," Marcia responded.

Rufus and Marcia sat in silence after finishing two donuts and two coffees that Rufus had picked up at the 24 hour 7-11 store at James River Blvd. on his way to the office.

And then a Ford van pulled in behind the building and did a U-turn and backed up against the back door entrance.

Rufus and Marcia watched silently as two men exited the vehicle and went into the store.

A bay door was opened, and the two men started unloading items from the van's rear storage – what looked to be like large boxes of non-perishable goods, but they were not heavy because neither man had trouble lifting the boxes.

Marcia asked for a camera, and Rufus handed her his. She opened the aperture a couple notches and adjusted the shutter speed to 1/8 second for the darkness of the morning and stabilized the camera on the dashboard. She took a picture of the one man unloading the goods on her side of the truck – and zoomed in on the face.

"That's Graemes," Marcia said.

"Excuse me. Say that again," Rufus said as he munching on a donut.

"That's Graemes, the guy who was driving the cargo van at the warehouse. And the other person is his partner Ortegan."

"Good to know," Rufus said nonchalantly.

"So they do drugs and counterfeit goods -- coming from the same source likely," Marcia said.

Rufus sat silent and now knew why he wanted Marcia with him. He reached in the back of the SUV and got a night vision video recorder. He opened the window and took several pictures of the men while they were unloading the vehicle.

Marcia said no more but thoughts were reeling in her mind about how Skooly was involved in organized crime throughout upper Hampton Roads – and that this area was an import and distribution point -- and just how involved it was with cops, judges, and politicians in the circle.

Marcia grabbed another donut. "They're good Rufus."

Rufus sighed at the men unloading the truck, "Got them at 7-11. I like the chocolate."

"The plain and cinnamon were great, and the coffee was good too. You married Rufus?" Marcia asked while chewing away.

"Once, but she didn't see much future with a clammer on the James River."

"Well, there lots of other women out there."

"There's lot of jobs too," Rufus said. "Been looking at the waitress at Rosie's."

"Well, if it's meant to happen, it will," Marcia said.

"Somehow that wording never satisfied me, but the donuts are good."

Marcia smiled while sitting and watching the two men unloading 20 boxes of fake goods.

"Let's drag this surveillance out for awhile and make some money, think about these things. Time has a way of solving puzzles."

"Might fix the waitress at Rosie's," Marcia.

"Might," Rufus said and smiled.

Marcia thought it would only take a short amount of time to report Attorney Skooly to the District Attorney for operating a criminal drug and counterfeit goods organization, but she wasn't about to utter a thing right now knowing an adversary was probably listening to her words. She started planning to get all the evidence and take it to Captain Tellis of the police department.

"They should be through shortly, so why don't you take the rest of the day off," Rufus said. "I'll do some paperwork at the office, and maybe tomorrow you can visit the pool again --- try to find out more about our lady friend," Rufus said.

"Sounds good. Okay to drink on the job?" Marcia asked.

"Can you hold your liquor?" Rufus asked.

"Can a fish swim?" Marcia asked.

"Not in its liquor," Rufus said, and they both smiled.

Rufus reached over to his glove compartment and pulled out a plastic kit that contained a brush, inkpad, dust in a bottle, and some tape.

"Let me guess," Marcia said as she looked on. "It's for sketching in case the camera doesn't work."

"No. It's a fingerprint kit, in case the police don't work."

"Cool. How does it work?"

"Put some dust on a print place and brush softly to reveal any print and either take a picture or lift them up with this here tape," Rufus said handling the tape.

"Let me see," Marcia said as she reached over and held each item.

"That there powder is just baby powder. You can use about anything," he said as he held a small bottle.

"Take it with you and practice some," Rufus said.

"Sure. Thanks Rufus. This job gets more interesting every day."

"Be real interesting now that we seen Gram and Oregano over there," Rufus said.

And Marcia bowed her head and put the kit in her purse.

"Just beware," Rufus said as he started up the vehicle and they went back to the office.

40.

When Marcia got out of the vehicle, she looked over at her car to see the left rear tire was nearly flat.

Rufus saw her stare and knew there was something wrong -- that someone more than likely let the air out. Only God knew what else had happened.

"Whaddaya think?" Rufus asked.

"Same person who's been bothering me, See what I've been talking about," Marcia said. "But this time he's really messed up," as she looked closer at the tire and a fingerprint visible on the tire lettering with the morning sun shining on it.

"Let's try out that fingerprint kit if you don't mind," Marcia said.

"Don't mind at all," Rufus said.

He got out of the vehicle and walked over to look at the print at the top corner of the tire lettering Marcia was looking at.

"Lord, you got good eyes," Rufus said.

"Eat a lot of chicken livers," Marcia said.

"Chicken livers good for the eyes?" Rufus asked as he stooped down to look closer.

"Good for anemia too. Got a lot of iron in them."

"A person can learn a lot on a job like this," Rufus added.

Marcia got the bottle of powder from the kit, opened the top and lightly brushed it on the print. If the print had been on the other side of the car, it would never have shown up.

"Perfect. Gimme the tape and get a picture of it," Rufus said.

Rufus taped the print and took it to the Toyota and taped it to some paper on the hood of the Toyota.

"Lord, you're good Rufus. How about the cap?"

"To the valve stem? Too ridged. Good thing you had a clean tire."

"Didn't want to disappoint Ms. Hendricks in case she walked to the parking lot at the swimming pool," Marcia said.

"I knew there was a reason I hired you."

"I put the $25.00 car wash on the expense account."

"Oh."

Rufus handed the paper to Marcia and told her to get to Tellis as soon as possible. "Take all the evidence and give it to him. We'll likely get canned from this job but I'm sure Starr Hendricks will keep us busy, if anything but to distract from something else."

"That, and our overseers," Marcia responded. "Okay. I'll see you in a couple days."

"And ask Tellis if he's got any jobs available while you're there," Rufus yelled out.

"For you or me?" Marcia.

"Both of us with this kind of action going on," Rufus said.

Marcia smiled and got into her vehicle.

Rufus stared at her car as she drove off and wondered just how this drama would end.

41.

Marcia drove slowly to the nearest gas station while her head was reeling: artificial light was hitting her face from somewhere above in the sky and it seemed like a car was coming at her every intersection.

Maybe the donuts had something to do with this, causing me to be paranoid, she thought.

A car also seemed to be following her but she had to stop and get air for sure.

She figured stopping at a place that was busy would be better than stopping at a deserted place. At least there would be some people around that might help her if there was trouble.

But at the Exxon station there were a couple of cars near the air pump.

So she went on to the next station, where there were no cars near an air pump.

Naomi told me not to get too excited when these coincidences happened – a lot of it was being remotely programmed over the community to make a victim feel paranoid.

She stopped at the station and was able to pump air in the tire without any trouble, other than being distracted by a vehicle which pulled into the parking lot and sat there.

She felt the tire for any nails or slow leaks but felt nothing, and the stem seemed to be in good shape, so she took off quickly towards home still mindful of the fingerprint paper and its place securely in her purse in a plastic bag. That would be her saving grace, or her doom if the print had no merit.

She arrived home at the apartment complex at 9:00 and waited for a couple of minutes in the parking lot to see that no one was following her.

She went into the apartment relieved that she made it safely, but then thought she had not checked her markers -- that they weren't there!

She sat down and said a little prayer and thanked God for life and wisdom. It was still a beautiful day and he was in control.

She would not be scared of evil. She did want to tell someone else what was happening, so she made a phone call to Richie and left a "hi" message that she was home and told him that someone had let the air out of a tire on her car. Just to make sure, she looked out the window at the car and the tire seemed to be fine, so there could not have been a leak.

Surely they have been in the apartment here also and they do not want me to go to the police, she was thinking.

As well as she could have left right then, she decided to wait and get her rest. The perpetrators would not control her agenda by getting her to run around everywhere in vain. She had a life to live.

But she would be careful what she ate. Naomi had told her that canned food would sometimes be tampered with, salt, condiments, or just anything the perpetrators knew their victims liked.

Marcia examined some canned beef, heard the air come from the can when it was opened, and made a macaroni dish with the beef for lunch.

Even the different size crimp rings on the top, sides, and bottom of cans were being picked up by some kind of radar to read the product and produce subliminal messaging. Then Marcia thought about the different designs on plastic bottles and wondered if artificial lights sources were determining the type of drink in a container a victim was drinking from.

Tomorrow she would see Tellis, if she was alive.

But Rufus would step in and get the evidence there surely. *Good to have someone else who knows about this*, she was thinking.

She ate and rested and thought about Starr at the pool and swimming. It was good to have a job, and good to know God.

42.

The targeting got worse in the evening and Marcia was getting a headache. She thought there was some kind of noise causing it.

She looked out the window and saw nothing suspicious. But then it almost seemed like the noise was in the house, so she walked over to the air conditioner fan, where it seemed louder. Naomi had said transformers were often the source of such noise and that every air conditioning unit has one.

Marcia put some cardboard in the window to see if that stopped it but there was no difference. Naomi had also said the perpetrators use the refrigerator condenser as an antenna through the electrical system to send subliminal messages; they might aim something at a window to get a person's vibrations off the pane, or they might have placed a transmitter in a person's residence.

It could be a host of things that Marcia did not know about.

Marcia got up and cleaned the kitchen and bathroom while looking for anything out of place.

After another frozen dinner, she got her clothes and bag packed for the next day at the pool, but first she would make her way to see Captain Tellis in the morning.

If she didn't get much sleep this night and wasn't able to think well in the morning, she would at least have the fingerprint sample and pictures of Graemes and Ortegan available along with the drug paraphernalia pictures ready to go to the police station.

She laid out her swimming suit. If she could just get through one more day, things would get better.

She was awakened at 3:30 a.m. Friday morning with a loud ringing in her ear, an abnormal light hitting her eyes, and some kind of banging that sounded like a door opening and shutting. She tried to get some rest by turning sideways on the bed, but her nerves were jangled. She got up to take a shower and checked her razor only to find someone had put old blades in the new slot. Earlier in the week, she had found dirty clothes mixed in with washed clothes. Then she realized the shampoo could be contaminated, so she used soap to wash her hair.

What else have they done? She thought as she was washing her hair. *Naomi said they built a bird's nest out of pine straw on the top of her car engine, which started a fire and could have killed her. Do I need to check these things?*

She finished showering and picked up a towel only to find a new hole in it.

She would not let these things deter her. She had her faith. She may be without any safe food or a stable place to live but she had her faith which no one could take from her.

And now she had some evidence of illegal activities. This was her day and no one would stop her.

Before dressing and lying back down for a little more sleep, she made sure her camera was packed also.

She lay down in the cool of the bedroom on top of the white sheets and said her prayers and drifted off to sleep

The dream came slowly, showing her drifting off a highway down onto an embankment where no one would find her. She had passed away from earth to an unknown place that was isolated and dark, and she thought of her family and Richie. The hypnosis waves continued to emanate until finally sunlight from the window brought her back to reality. And she thought about what had happened and knew it to be some kind of artificial telepathy dream, completely programmed to make her think she would die in an accident.

And she prayed it off.

God was in control of her life and he would prevail this day because of her prayers to glorify him.

She awoke and praised God and gave thanks for his presence and intervention. The day outside was sunny and clear, and Marcia hoped it would stay that way for the afternoon poolside meeting with Starr Hendricks.

Marcia had selected a bright flowered print skirt with an ivory pullover knit boat shirt but she was breathing hard as she put the clothing on. The energy was bothering her nerves, which constricted the muscles, and caused stress on the lungs and organs; they were not getting the oxygen they needed. Maybe she was implanted – she didn't know – but regardless, today she would take that evidence to the police station.

For precaution, she went to the cabinet and got a charcoal tablet, opened it, and spread some on a cracker to neutralize any poisons that she may have had. Marcia had learned about the healing value of natural foods and herbs from her boyfriend years ago. Keeping the body in harmony with alkaline foods went a long way towards having good health. This was not the time to be weak in faith, nor strength, so she would continue in prayers and eat the necessary fats, oils, and protein she needed for life – and the purer – the better.

She plugged her refrigerator cord back in the socket after leaving it out at night, grabbed her bags of safe snacks, notebook, and camera.

She walked to the door to mark it, lock it, and go to the car, looking around as she went. She got in the car and backed out slowly onto the street. *Probably already have the police in their back pockets*, she thought as she drove to the station, *but Rufus said Tellis is okay.*

It was 10:00 a.m. and Marcia pulled into the police station parking lot and parked in a vacant spot. She was shaking a bit as she got out of the car, seeing the police vehicles and wondering what she had got herself into. She had to be business like going into that station, as her head was still reeling from the night's lack of sleep.

She opened and walked by the metal reinforced front door, past the ticket paying counter and to the counter where she used to deliver depositions. She asked the clerk behind the counter to see Capt. Tellis. The clerk nodded, walked around the corner and came back and motioned her to walk through the passageway and to the right hallway. She found the office and walked through the doorway.

"Well, if ain't Ms. Perry Mason. Thugs still bothering you?"

"How'd you know?"

"I'm the police chief. I know everything."

"No thugs but a deceptive sneaky no-good stalker who follows me around sabotaging my goods."

Tellis sat back in his gray swivel chair and stared at Marcia. "And just what goods have been desecrated?"

"Air was let out of my tire," Marcia replied.

"And Joe the beggar on 10th had his cup stolen the other day," the chief responded. "Look lady, there are 217 bench warrants sitting there on the delivery desk, out of state murderers are hiding somewhere along the bay, and a rapist who likes young kids has suddenly vanished from police custody. And you got some air let out of your tire." Tellis sat back in his chair staring at her.

Marcia was not about to be intimidated or frightened. "Captain Tellis, I'm not here to pacify your job function.

221

I'm here reporting a stalker, thief, and covert assailant who is using communication and surveillance devices for uses otherwise than what they are intended to be used – and who defames, slanders, and hurts me with something– and three men who are distributing a boat load of heroin from a warehouse at the water's edge to places up and down the east coast along with counterfeit goods that likely amounts to several million dollars of cash. Now I can stand here and waste my time with you or walk over to the District Attorney's Office down the street and give him this evidence. What's it going to be?"

Tellis straightened up in his chair a little and put his hands on his desk.

"Alright, just hold on. Let me see what you got," the Captain said as he did not want any part of a District Attorney inquiry.

"First, here's a fingerprint of the no-good's hand on my tire," said Marcia as she laid the paper with the taped powdered print in front of him. Find out whose print this is. Second, here are pictures of the men at the warehouse and a building of counterfeits goods, along with drug paraphernalia pictures. And here are pictures of the transport vehicle and some copies of the drivers' criminal records."

Marcia stepped back from the desk and waited with her arms crossed and shouldering her hand bag.

"Okay, I'll get the print researched. How do you know a boat came in to the warehouse?"

"Water. Salt water was seeping from back of the cargo van. They deliver first of the month I suspect," Marcia said.

"We'll stake it out. How's Rufus?" the Captain asked.

"Nervous and he asked if you have any jobs available," Marcia responded.

"Well, Not right at the moment but I'll keep him in mind. And you?"

"I'm following a woman around a swimming pool and enjoying the sunshine."

"Got a bullet proof bathing suit?" the captain quizzed and smiled.

"Don't need one. This one distracts men from shooting and makes women somber with envy," as she knew Tellis had been looking at her colored visible shoulder straps the entire time she was there.

She took out one of the business cards Rufus had given her and put it on the desk. "When you get the print identified, call me."

And she walked out of the office relieved and happy.

She exited the police station and got in the car and drove straight to Riley's Delicatessen where she knew she could get a sandwich --- and some ice cream.

43.

In Bougainville, Brahaim was observing Marcia with interest knowing the operation in Newport News was going down despite Skooly's influence over area law enforcement and blackmailed thugs.

Skooly had picked on the wrong person this time.

But Marcia could be eliminated by an accident or something. It was the something that had eluded Marcia up to now, with poisonous drugs in her food, low air tire pressure designed to make her run off the road, and remote energy to get her to commit suicide. Nothing was working, and it wasn't the organization's policy to directly kill anyone.

But something had to be done to stop or slow her down.

There was enough evidence and talk between Rufus Stronger, Marcia's boyfriend, and the cops to find out about drug shipments, counterfeit goods, and Skooly's clients.

Even Whitten, the owner of the storage facilities could be held liable for housing criminal activity and conspiring to sell drugs and counterfeit goods.

Brahaim knew the Premier would be blamed for failure to control the situation – he would be canned and exiled to a poor country with no benefits.

Brahaim got up nervously from his chair and walked around the room waiting for Johnny to show up and take over the controls. He looked out the lone window of the mountainside cave and wondered about his own future and living in shadows the rest of his life -- or getting a decent job and raising a family. Maybe it was time for a switch, even if he was targeted for assassination.

He said nothing when the Premiere walked in for the night shift but grabbed a coat off a nearby table, signed a check-out register, and walked out the door to the fresh air of the ocean. Maybe he should just keep walking to the dock, take the first boat to the mainland and find his way back to Yemen – before something bad really happened.

But the guards would see him and report him to Johnny, and Brahaim might make it as far to the airport in Melbourne and be killed.

44.

Marcia arrived at Riley's and ordered a Pastrami, Cheese, and Fried Tomato sandwich with lettuce on the side along with some potato wedges.

The sandwich was on black rye bread, and Marcia thought it was very good.

She thought about how situations in the world related to the Bible and now she was thinking about the wording *very good.*

God made a lot of things in five days and saw that they were good, but when he made man and woman on the sixth day, he said it was very good. I hope I'm very good at whatever it is God wants me to do.

The pastrami filled her need for pork, which she had regularly as a teenager after searching for something in an empty refrigerator and cabinet. But usually there were some cans of Vienna sausage and pork and beans stowed away on a back shelf in a closet.

She had read somewhere that pork gives energy, and energy was something she needed, after all the stress she had been through lately.

She sat awhile longer and thought about Starr and the pool area – knowing she had to get some information from her. She thought about the questions that needed to be asked, without being too invasive.

She got a cup of butter pecan ice cream at the checkout register and paid her bill.

She got into her car and drove to the country club all the time mindful of anyone following her. From now on, she would also be aware of any waiter or waitress at a restaurant drugging her food after hearing Naomi's warning about the issue.

It was a warm day and cars filled the parking lot at the country club. Marcia thought maybe it was because it was Friday and some people took off work early.

She parked the car and walked through the enclave to the attendant's counter and showed her identification badge. She exchanged greetings with some bystanders and got a key to a storage bin to put her belongings.

Looking out into the pool area, she did not see Starr, but it was still early.

Marcia went to the locker room and changed into her bathing suit -- and made sure the little recorder would fit just inside the padded lining, and then she took it back out.

She brushed her hair quickly and locked up her outerwear in the locker.

On the way out of the locker area, she grabbed a couple of towels and went to find a vacant lounge chair to get some rest.

Last night had been extremely difficult with something causing her body to ache. She twisted most of the night trying to get comfortable but nothing worked. She could only guess the perpetrators were sending pulsed microwave energy through the antenna towers and dishes.

She had felt the energy pulsing at the police station also, but there were also nearby transformers on utility poles and a host of electronic equipment in the station.

Marcia felt less energy in a community that had underground utilities and enclosed transformers, but they were neighborhoods near the beach, where utilities installed wiring underground to escape hurricane damages.

After thirty minutes, Marcia cooled off under a tall outdoor sprinkler head. Drying with her towel, she went to sit by some other people that had now come into the pool area.

Marcia thought maybe she wouldn't get targeted as bad if she was around other people. Maybe the system wouldn't know who was who. But intermingling with other folk is healthy, and Marcia liked meeting new people.

Two young women were chatting away and Marcia found a chaise lounge chair near them and introduced herself, which would also dispel any notions that Marcia was there just to see Starr.

In fifteen minutes Marcia was asleep, having been exhausted from the last 48 hours. She awoke 20 minutes later to see Starr in her usual place.

If Starr came over and talked, fine, but Marcia wasn't going to force the issue. Her thoughts were confused enough. Her muscles were hurting from the targeting and she just wanted to lie in the sun and go for a swim. Depressed and lonely, she drifted back off to sleep.

After waking and still not wanting to talk to Starr or much less investigate her, Marcia gathered her belongings from the locker and walked out to the car and drove home.

Next time, she thought. *There's plenty of time to find out about Starr. I need to set my own house in order right now.*

She felt miserable. She went into her apartment and threw her stuff down frustrated that she was still being bothered. Today, she didn't care if someone had entered the apartment or not. It was the end of the week and she'd work on Starr next week.

She wondered about her life. She sat doing nothing for hours until Richie called.

And she answered the phone, "Hello."

"Hi. How are you?"

"Very tired. I got hurt again last night," she responded.

"It's still going on, huh?"

"Is. But at least I got to the police and turned in some evidence about my stalker."

"What kind of evidence?"

"A finger print, and some pictures of the warehouse workers, who coincidentally are the same people delivering counterfeit goods to a store Rufus is watching."

"Wow. This has all the makes of a thriller movie.'

"There's more – the two workers were clients of Skooly."

"Oh, so there's a conspiracy to harass and shut you up, maybe even forever."

"Yep. Tellis told me to lay low but I think I'll let my stalkers know exactly what I'm doing -- trying to put them in jail and get their drugs dumped in the river," Marcia said boldly. "If I'm still alive."

Richie listened intently judging whether he wanted to hear her drama or not, but he did care about her, and he was in a position to help if there was a legal matter. He knew exactly how evil lawyers could be when it came to making a dollar. Now maybe it was his turn to put a couple away for good, even though he was blacklisted in another county.

"Okay. So what's in store for the weekend?" Richie asked.

"I don't know what's in the store but I know what's in the kitchen. Very little."

"Is that a hint?" Richie asked.

"It's a fact."

"Okay. How about tomorrow after golf?"

"Can't disturb your golf game."

Richie blushed somewhat and meekly said yes. He tried to ignore her response but knew she would win despite his best strategy to pacify her.

"It's your day. Give me a call and I'll be there," he said.

"Play golf and give me a call afterwards," she responded.

Richie said, "Okay, Thanks. Who knows? Maybe I'll be playing with a judge who can help out."

"Got one of them right here," Marcia responded.

Richie had to think about that too for a second, and he figured he was just getting in more trouble the more he talked, so he finally said, "You do, don't you? Talk tomorrow." And Richie terminated the call.

Richie sat silently in his study at home thinking about Marcia and her problems. The room began to close. It shut him down. But he would not be held hostage to silence in the midst of oppression and intimidation upon Marcia – like what happened to him in Virginia Beach. Nor would he be held hostage to judges who were being bribed by lawyers to get favorable verdicts for their clients and monetary awards that were unjustified.

Marcia was right about his golf game taking priority over helping disadvantaged and oppressed people. Sure his law practice was helping people who had been victimized by bad products, but what about the people who were out to hurt other people, using positions of authority to get their way, which he knew violated the law. Politicians and law enforcement personnel often violated the section of law in Title 18 that restricted them from using their positions to harass people. And he knew he could do something about it. He had represented several people in civil rights lawsuits against government over reach when he first started practicing law.

But would they come after him again? Like the time he was working in Virginia Beach and a private hearse began to ride around his residence, his car sabotaged, and his reputation in the legal community ruined by lies and defamation. Reporting these extraneous events to the F.B.I. did no good, but if any good came out of it, he made some friends in the bureau, and just maybe Anna Kalestrom could stop the technological targeting of Marcia.

He could avoid this confrontation again by simply walking away from Marcia.

But would such a drama occur later in his life?

How long could he keep running away? And would it affect his willingness to live a confident happy life knowing he failed to confront evil when it involved the very person who made him happy?

It would be no problem to file conspiracy charges against Skooly. He knew Skooly would fold quickly, since he was ready to retire.

But was that the way to get the woman he cared about -- when there were hidden people using technology to disturb her? But then Skooly was the connection, and Richie knew he had the power to at least subpoena and interrogate him.

The room lightened up, or was it his mind? He stared at the law books on the shelf, the street outside the paned window, and the papers and pens on his desk wondering about his life and future. Marcia lived a care free and righteous life willing to take risks to help the oppressed. What kind of condition would humanity be in if no one confronted evil and perpetrators were allowed to roam free to drug kids, use technology to target people, and disturb the physical and mental health of citizens?

He could be writing his own death sentence by filing charges against Skooly -- but he could just be an associate submitting evidence of the stalking connection to the district attorney prosecutor.

That would help Marcia fight back against the criminal enterprise she had somehow become a victim of. And maybe he was a victim also.

The sun began to set and darkness again invaded the room, but this time it wasn't mental darkness – it was earthly darkness.

He got up from his chair, walked across the mosaic tiled floor of the study area to the living room, and for the first time since he faced ungodly fear at the law practice on the other side of the river – he began to pray and silently voice his concerns to God. After a few minutes, he felt peace.

He went back to the study and began to write a complaint against Jon Skooly's firm for defamation, stalking, and coercion.

He would telephone Anna Monday morning in reference to the high-tech targeting.

He wasn't fighting for Marcia; he was fighting for himself.

45.

It was Friday night and Marcia did not feel like doing anything special. She would relax and have some peace knowing that she had reported her stalker to the police. And besides, she had a job offer by Tellis that could amount to a career position with benefits.

And there was Richie – the anchor of her life when she was down and out. She had tomorrow to look forward to.

The pool visit did her good: her skin was tanning, she felt balanced, and though events surrounding her seemed dismal, physically she was fine.

But her happiness was short lived when she walked into the kitchen and poured a glass of water and put some ice in it only to see something rise to the top. She sipped it, and it tasted metallic.

God, have they done something to my water also, or to my kitchen spigot? Well, it won't work, she was thinking.

Her next thought was that plumbers may have worked on the water pipes while she was away, but the apartment manager had not given notice of such action.

Then Marcia remembered Naomi telling her perpetrators had unscrewed the little filter on the end of her kitchen spigot, poisoned it, and put it back on.

Being safe, Marcia reached up into the cabinet and took a charcoal capsule out of a plastic container and opened it – she put the charcoal on a cracker and ate it, and she felt the powder neutralizing the water.

What else have they done while I was away? And where can I get water?

She emptied the glass and walked into the bathroom to open the bath faucet and fill it.

She tasted it, and it was fine.

Problem solved. *With God, there was always a way to make things work*, she would think. She bowed her head for a moment and gave thanks. As little as a problem it was, it could have been huge.

She checked out the cans of food in the cabinet. She looked at the tops for any residue, and the labels for any foreign substance.

From what Naomi said, the perps were using some kind of radar to scope out the rings on the top and bottom of the cans, so the system would know what kind of food was in whatever can. If the sound of air wasn't noticeable when opening a can, it was probably drugged.

And the plastic containers, with all those swirls in the plastic – signified what kind of drink or substance was in there.

If that wasn't enough, Naomi had told her the perpetrators often go to the food store knowing what items their victims ate, to drug the foods.

If there was only one item on the shelf, Naomi said to leave it alone: it was bad. If taken, the perpetrators would know if she took it. If she didn't take it, the perpetrators would easily buy that one item back so another person wouldn't get sick by mistake.

Naomi had figured these things out because she had gotten sick to the stomach on several occasions and didn't know why – until she came home one day and saw that several can foods that were missing were now back in the cabinet.

Naomi said, "Above all, make sure your bedroom door is locked and braced before you sleep. The perpetrators try to tire their victims out for a couple days prior and then silently enter the room in the middle of the night and inject neurotoxins in the ear canal. And you should really carry some of your food with you; especially salt, because they know a person uses that every day. Always mark your door when leaving. If it gets to the point they know your every move, then tell someone you're going to one place that is not too important, and then go to wherever you had planned to go in the first place. The system picks up all our conversations, so just speak into the phone to a friend or a recording at a business about your false destination."

"But I can't lie," Marcia had responded.

"You're lying to a machine that is using artificial technology trying to kill you," she had said. "God understands."

Marcia had a lot to learn about how to keep safe but she was making progress at living a normal life: foregoing baked goods with baking powder in them; being in safe areas; recording anyone that was following her, and telling trustworthy friends what was happening to her. The perpetrators could take her goods and defame her, but they couldn't take her faith and witness.

Marcia sat in a living room chair thinking about things and what she could do to find more peace. She knew the system was now targeting appliances, furniture and bed mattress springs, and even the screws in the floor underlayment. There were several programs in the C.I.A.'s history that recorded the radiation frequencies of stoves, wash machines, toilets, and furniture.

When is this going to stop?, she asked herself. *Or is it a programmed situation?*

She had recently read a book about some silent sound technology that the devil was using to try and convince people it was God talking to them and getting them to rob stores, commit lewd acts, and kill themselves.

The system would not work on Christians, and Marcia figured out the difference; she could tell that energies were pulsing word connotations to her voice box and thoughts.

Marcia went back to the kitchen and found some safe canned food to make a salmon rice dish with some Monterey Jack cheese and tomato.

The energy was continuing to bother her but she decided to live her life freely and normally as possible, and who knows, Captain Tellis may be right on her perpetrator's doorstep.

She would go to bed early and look forward to Saturday seeing Richie.

In the morning, she'd wash some clothes and go get a haircut at The Style Shop on Main Street. She'd stop by a discount store to buy more can foods – a store where the perps would least expect her.

To rest tonight, she'd cover her head with her Bible and trust in God to save her. Maybe the lead inked pages would help.

Across the street from Marcia's apartment, Julian Muestro looked on fitfully knowing Marcia had gone to the police station and talked to the Captain.

He worried about what might have been said, and he wondered if he had left any clues of his stalking around Marcia's apartment. He went over everything in his mind, from the time he took some of her clothes and personal documents to the time he'd follow her around and spied on her across from the warehouse in a storage unit.

He had returned most of her food after he drugged it, and he had been very careful about not leaving any trace of his entrance into her apartment.

What could he have done to not leave a trail? Did someone see him? And now he began to think about packing up and leaving town.

If Skooly found out though, he was dead.

He didn't care. He would leave the state regardless of probationary requirements; he'd rather be in trouble with the law than Skooly. At least he'd be protected somewhat in prison. But tonight, he would not aim anything at her or the apartment – he was scared – and a policeman had been patrolling the street this afternoon.

46.

Marcia slept through the night and awoke at 7:00 --
amazed her sleep had not been interrupted.

Maybe something has finally stopped, she thought.

The sheet was still on her and there didn't seem to be
any new marks on her body. She had found a small pin
prick behind her right ear weeks ago, and she was still
wondering about it.

She lay awhile longer enjoying some peace.

After her prayers, she got up and showered with an
earth soap that was made of lard, lye, and a little
seaweed. It smelled like wintergreen, and she lathered
her skin with it neutralizing some of the damage from the
radiation.

*Seaweed removes radiation from the inside, I hope it
does from the outside also*, she was thinking as she

scrubbed away a few dark spots that had appeared at the base of her feet. *Naomi had said these were some kind of neurotoxins that find their way to the feet. Thank God for Naomi.*

Marcia finished showering and dressed in brown slacks and a halter top knowing some of her hair would usually end up on her clothes as much as Lauren would try to keep it off.

Marcia arrived at the small shop on Main Street in Newport News just before 10:00 and took a chair by an upright stand with a fern plant drooping over its sides. Lauren and Marcia exchanged greetings while Lauren was finishing up trimming a woman's hair.

After ten minutes, Marcia went and sat in the unoccupied chair and let Lauren put the apron around her shoulders

Marcia relaxed while Lauren was sweeping the floor and gathering up loose strands of hair from the previous cut.

Marcia wondered just how much control the perpetrators would have over Lauren cutting her hair. Naomi had warned her about such crazy things – the targeting getting a hair stylist to cut hair crooked or leave splotches.

Naomi said perpetrators had control over emergency services personnel, military functions, law enforcement agencies, and government contractors, synchronizing their movements around a victim to make a victim look and seem crazy, like when Naomi would drive into a gas station parking area and a song would play over the outside speakers that would mimic her life. She'd pull out of the station and then an ambulance would be in front of her. If the ambulance turned off the road – a helicopter would appear over the horizon – all synchronized electronically to try and make a victim paranoid and want to take drugs and end up in a mental health treatment house or hospital.

Marcia didn't believe her at first but she did now, after experiencing such action.

"How's it going Lauren?" Marcia asked.

"Fine, fine. And you?"

"Doing well."

Lauren didn't speak much and Marcia didn't force the issue, as Marcia again was just enjoying some peace and rest sitting in the chair.

After the trim, Marcia looked in the mirror to see if her hair looked okay, tapered along the sides and back, just above the shoulders. It would be cool enough for the hot summer months.

She paid the bill and walked out of the shop feeling better.

She went back home and finished some cleaning and read some magazines about vegetable gardens and wildlife on the peninsula.

Today, she would turn on the computer to check mail and real news from true news stations.

Richie picked Marcia up at 5:00 and they went to Johnny Bourellis Seafood House on the Chesapeake Bay for dinner.

The place looked more like a house than a restaurant. There was no large parking lot or fancy front porch, and it was at the end of a neighborhood that had Cape Cod style houses.

There was an herb garden on the side that was enclosed with a white picket fence. A concrete patio sat off to the side of the garden at the back of the house.

It was quiet there because there was no vehicle traffic at this dead end road – just the hum from an occasional passing boat or chirps from sea gulls.

Now it was early evening and candle lights would adorn each table on white tablecloths with crystal glasses and silverware for dinner.

Marcia and Richie were escorted to a booth with red vinyl coverings that looked like something in a tavern, but it was very private as the backs of the seats reached well above a person's shoulders.

The selections were simple dishes: Fried Scallops, Oysters, Flounder, Crab cakes or Clam dinners with choice of potatoes, slaw, and hushpuppies.

But a unique pre-dinner entrée made Bourellis special - - a fresh loaf of homemade bread would be put on every table with a bowl of melted butter and shrimp with a side sauce. Those items were a dinner itself.

Richie spoke up after as they looked at the menus. "Most menus usually have such small wording but not here. The small print, always something to watch out for," he said as a suspicious lawyer would.

Marcia said, "Well, it's a beautiful place here and cozy." She took off her blue sweater and laid it on the seat. "What are you having?"

"The large fried seafood platter, it's got everything."

"I'll have the scallops with the salad," Marcia said.

She quietly set the menu down -- still amazed there was peace and quiet in her mind after a week of turmoil.

But she would not be letting her guard down, and she worried a about the waiter serving the food even though he was nice when taking orders.

Richie had a beer and Marcia had a White Chablis wine to drink. She certainly wanted to keep her senses but a small glass of wine wouldn't hurt.

"You're quiet tonight," Richie said.

"There is peace in the valley," Marcia said with a sly smile.

"Oh. Things have quieted down?" Richie asked.

"Seems like it," Marcia said, wanting to change the subject.

Marcia bowed her head ashamed of her problems but she continued talking. "There is some good news: Capt. Tellis is investigating the fingerprint and sending a patrol around."

"That's great, and a complaint is going to the D.A." Richie responded.

"By who?" Marcia asked satirically.

Richie said, "The magic man."

"Richie Granger, you got tricks up your sleeve?" Marcia asked.

Richie just nodded slightly.

244

"You're helping me in this?" Marcia asked, as a few tears came to her eyes.

"You bet. Which is more important? I thought. Golf or you?" He waited to see her expressionless face and finally started confessing something he had needed to talk about for a long time. "It bothered me about what was happening to you. I did some research and found there are other victims also. The least I can do is help the person I care about more than anything in the world."

Marcia's eyes swelled with more tears and she reached over to cover Richie's hand.

He continued, "At some time in life, a person has got to stand up for what is right, regardless of the threats or people doing evil. I've been running away from that too long, and this is not only something to help you but me and my faith."

"Well, thank you, Richie. I need all the support I can get right now. God will bless you."

But she knew her situation was grave with the high tech weaponry taking place on her life: it was probably more than even a trial lawyer could handle. She had heard of two lawyers that had lost their license to practice law.

The waiter arrived with the food and Marcia slightly smiled at him as he lay down the plates.

After the waiter left, Richie said, "They got a herb garden in the back," Richie said.

"I like herbs, got some parsley growing on the side of the front porch."

"So what's up for next week and Starr Hendricks?" Richie asked.

"Richie, you know that's confidential investigator information," Marcia said.

"Oh. What wouldn't be confidential?" he said.

"I'll show you later," Marcia said.

"Okay," Richie said nodding his head while planning his next golf outing, knowing Marcia was under stress. He did not want to push her into anything she didn't feel like talking about.

After they finished dinner, Richie dropped her off at her apartment, and they were content to have Sunday apart from each other.

Monday morning at 10:00 Marcia's phone rang and she picked up the handset to listen.

"Is this Marcia?"

"It is," Marcia answered sullenly, figuring there was more bad news in her life.

"Got good news," he said.

"What kind of good news, and who are you?" she asked.

"Tellis. Got an I.D. on that print."

"And whose I.D. is it?"

"Guy named Muestro. Julian Muestro, been charged with robbery recently," Tellis said as he looked over the booking report sitting on his office desk. "Breaking and entering a commercial business," he finished.

"Muestro? Was he prosecuted?" Marcia asked.

"Got probation," Tellis said.

"Represented by who?" Marcia.

"Jon Skooly."

"Well, that figures. That is where and when my trouble started with this stalking. I knew the man was involved somehow."

"Not the first time, but he always seems to get away with it unless one of his employees or clients files suit against him," Tellis commented.

"Well, I was an employee!" Marcia exclaimed.

Tellis said nothing, knowing he would open up another can of trouble if he found what happened between Skooly and Marcia, so he waited for Marcia to say something else.

It took Marcia a few more seconds to comprehend what was happening between Skooly and his clients. Skooly was foregoing attorney's fees to blackmail clients and target people he either didn't like or was scared to be sued by. Muestro was the client probably being blackmailed to stalk and watch her.

"Captain, Thank you. Do you know where this guy Muestro lives?"

"Right across the street from you," he answered. After a pause he continued, "I'm sending a man over there to ask some questions but we want to watch him for awhile, and I'll get back to you."

"Oh Jesus thank you! I'll be watching too!"

"You've done your investigating work well. Let us handle it, and if you would think about joining the department, let us know. But you would have to sign up for a few criminal justice courses at the school first."

"Well, let me think about it, and thanks again. You've made my day better. I was feeling very insecure and scared."

"Okay. I'll let you know of any new developments." Captain Tellis terminated the call and left Marcia with a silent receiver.

She put the phone down softly into its cradle, turned on the sofa to look around the room and thought about what had just transpired: her stalker is across the street, drugs were being traded at the warehouse, counterfeit goods were being stocked in a building, and worse, she was still being targeted electronically with ringing in her ear and some kind of pulsing to her nervous system. But now she had some hope to find out who, what, where, and why.

She called and left Richie a message that Captain Tellis had identified Julian Muestro as her stalker and that she had found out Skooly's cronies were attorneys of record in a criminal case representing Muestro.

She wanted to put Skooly in jail for life for ruining her career and health. She would report him to the Bar Association and gather more information for the Federal District Attorney to prosecute him for international drug trafficking, stalking, and undue coercion over her life. She wanted his phone calls monitored to find the connection between her electronic targeting.

But for now, she would be patient until more information was gathered to find out the source of his contacts.

But she felt victory, and she went to the kitchen and pulled out a cold cut sandwich from the refrigerator and began to eat. And she had a cup of tea using bottled water.

Finally, she thought. *Some help.*

Marcia got on the phone and called Stronger at the office. "Rufus, Captain says a guy named Julian Muestro is stalking me!"

"Heavens forbid. Good work. They going after him?"

"Not yet. They want to watch awhile. He lives across the street from me!"

"How convenient. Maybe we should get him first. Got an address?"

"No. Tellis says to stay out of it for now."

"Okay, but this is good. Ready for some more work?"

"Besides watching Ms. Hendricks?" Marcia said.

"We can do both, because Starr only visits the pool a couple times a week, and besides, we may have enough information for the mister to be satisfied," Rufus said.

"Okay. Now that I've got some relief from this crazy situation. What else you got?" Marcia asked.

"Got a call from a guy from the Democratic Party chairman."

"Oh, and what does he want?"

"Some dirt on a Republican legislator."

"Well, I'm not doing that Rufus. They're all dirty!"

"They may be, but the money is still green. And no, not this one. It's Reginald Wallis, and he's as straight as they come," Rufus responded.

"Well, whose side are we on?"

"His, but the legislator doesn't have to know. We just keep him happy feeding a little information."

"I think I understand. Make some money. Like what kind of information though?"

"Who Wallis is meeting in his office, who he's talking to, and find out if there are any problems at home."

"Sounds okay. It's a job and part of investigative work."

"Hey, one of these characters may become your best friend!"

"Or my worst enemy. I thought you were my best friend."

"I'm your boss. Business and intimacy don't mix."

"Glad you told me that. I won't spend any money on donuts."

Rufus said, "Well, there is that."

"Could be, except for you eating so many," Marcia responded.

Rufus smiled and said goodbye.

47.

Richie spent most of Monday morning researching inactive case files at the Circuit Court clerk's office for any product liability opportunities. He found two cases where seat belts failed to restrain occupants in vehicles and the insurance companies covered property loss and personal injuries of the victims but the seat belt companies were never held liable.

Richie returned to his office after lunch and retrieved Marcia's message from the answering machine -- about the police identifying Julian Muestro as her stalker – and that Skooly had represented Muestro in a criminal case.

Richie sat and thought about it.

If the police were investigating Muestro and suspected Skooly was involved, the D.A. would prosecute Skooly for criminal solicitation, if it could be proved Skooly had blackmailed Muestro.

But Julian Muestro would have to confess as such, and that would be highly unlikely.

If Richie did nothing, Skooly would surely continue his assault on Marcia trying to shut her up.

So what was he to do?

The Lawyer's Bar association wouldn't help because Skooly had friends there. Besides; it often took months to discipline a lawyer after written notices, hearings, and appeal procedures. A lot of things could happen in those months.

Maybe he could personally file charges of undue coercion and harassment against Skooly. But then the old man had judges on his side and that could turn out to be a circus.

He'd give Skooly a phone call -- let him know the problem -- and tell him to get off Marcia's back.

It was time to take action, and if something happened this time to him, it just would. There would be no running away from evil this time.

So he picked up the phone and called, and a secretary transferred him to Skooly.

In old school talk, Richie said, "Make a deal with you."

There was a pause for several seconds as Skooly thought about who was calling and what it was about.

He knew Richie was a newcomer to the area but also knew he wasn't a criminal lawyer and had no pending cases with him.

So Skooly said, "Okay."

"Get off Marcia Lemay's back and there'll be no trouble," Richie said.

Skooly normally would not have yielded to such a threat but this was different – Richie was bold and must know something, he thought.

Skooly began to feel the heat of the authorities catching him at covert activities the moment Johnnie had called from New Guinea last week.

Maybe it's time to quit, he thought. *I've got enough money to retire, and who needs the aggravation.*

For the first time in years, Skooly would yield to an upcoming brash lawyer, and he said, "Okay."

Richie said nothing and put down the telephone receiver and was actually amazed at his success. He smiled a little but would not glory in it, knowing Skooly had connections and could do some dirty things. Time would tell.

Skooly sat at his desk and mused over his achievement letters and diplomas on the wall: passing the bar examination after attending the University of Virginia, forming a law practice with three other attorneys and representing clients in family, civil, and criminal courts, and arguing cases before the State Supreme Court.

He had a good life outside the legal profession also: sailing around Cape Horn on a month long sabbatical, forming a young men's soccer league, and taking trips to the Caribbean Islands several times to visit friends at their seaside villas to play tennis, golf, and shuffleboard.

Though his marriages failed, he had three grandchildren whom he would not give up for anything.

But on the downside, he found himself taking out anger on his clients, when he saw how happy and successful they would be after his representation.

Jealousy ate at him. Why couldn't he have such a carefree attitude as his clients, he asked himself.

Now his world was crashing. Somewhere along life's line he had made bad choices. His power over people now got him the object of jealousy or hate. Or maybe it was revenge.

It was time to get out. He was 76 years old and his face had lost its shine. More than anything, a competitive desire to be the best, just wasn't there.

48.

Skooly got up from his chair and stuck his head past a
door jamb into an adjoining office where his associate
Blaine Fenton sat.

Blaine was staring at a telephone book, probably
thinking about looking up an address of his next victim,
since Blaine was the new man in the firm and serving an
initiation period of one year doing dirty work.

Skooly nodded at Blaine to follow him, and they headed
to the Courthouse Café across the street.

They sat down at a booth, and Skooly said he would be
quitting the firm: it was time to get out.

Blaine was not surprised. He had often wondered if he
was being groomed to take Skooly's place. The old man
was quiet lately – and making more mistakes than ever,
failing to serve proper notice of court motions to opposing

attorneys and file discovery documents with the clerk's office.

Skooly asked for Blaine's phone and punched in numbers for Vernon Hitchen's cell phone at the C.I.A. Headquarters in Washington D.C.

Vernon answered quietly on the fourth ring, "Yes?"

Skooly said his case was closed.

Vernon said, "Are you sure?"

Skooly gave his final code word of sincerity, "Absolutely."

Vernon had been a school buddy of Skooly's in college and majored in electrical engineering. He joined the C.I.A. as a cartography assistant and then worked his way into the human resources department – where he discovered job application files being kept on private citizens and their families.

He eventually forwarded many of those names to Zenithe's cell managers throughout the United States.

The citizens would be targeted by stalkers in liaison with contacts at the U.S. Air Force and Department of Energy under the guise of secret behavior modification programs such as MK-Ultra, which was funded by the U.S. Government and targeted unwitting citizens and Native Americans with remote neural monitoring, covert drugs, and radiation.

Skooly terminated the call and handed the phone back to Blaine. Skooly bowed his head for a moment and looked stoic.

Blaine understood what was happening, and now he wondered whether he wanted any part of this transfer of power. He sat looking at a glass of water before him.

Skooly told him to go back to the office, and he would see him later.

Skooly got up and exited the café and walked straight to Fintech Savings & Loan to withdraw $50,000.

Skooly may have made some bad choices in life but withdrawing money from Zenithe's account wouldn't be one of them.

After Skooly had exited the café, a man on a bar stool slowly turned to see where he was going.

Stan Kurchin, an undercover U.S. marshal sent by the F.B.I. to monitor Skooly's actions after a warrant had been signed by a judge at the Federal District Court, subtly looked at Skooly walking down the sidewalk.

Stan had been looking straight ahead at a mirror fronting the café's counter reflecting the images of Skooly and Blaine.

That incoming call from the Premiere in Bougainville to Skooly a week earlier had caught the fed's attention, along with Marcia's complaint to Captain Tellis, and Richie's informal conversations with friendly attorneys.

As soon as both Blaine and Skooly had left the café, Stan pulled a cell phone from his coat pocket and called Martin Stocholm at the F.B.I. office in Washington.

"He's made a call, using another phone," Stan said.

Martin asked, "Location?"

Stan gave the address of the café and the time the call was made.

257

There had also been multiple complaints to the F.B.I. about Skooly's actions from judges, politicians, and court appointed commissioners, who were complaining about Skooly's team threatening them in some way over legal matters.

The F.B.I. had relationships with telecom companies to trace local phone calls.

Stocholm called an AT&T company technical support officer and asked for an emergency location service for a telephone call made from the Courthouse Café in Newport News, Virginia, at 11:47 a.m.

After the request was made, Stocholm sat at his desk wondering just how much power Skooly had, for his own life could be in danger. Skooly was guilty of something or he wouldn't be using a friend's phone in a café just shortly after getting a call from Richie Granger and being confronted with a stalking charge.

Within an hour, Stocholm got the telephone number and name of Vernon Hichens, who worked at the Human Resources department of the C.I.A. Hichens would have access to personnel files and records of military personnel and their families with the Department of Defense upon background checks.

Marcia Lemay's father was in the Navy. He was a nuclear fission expert who had been stationed on the nuclear powered submarine Scorpion, and Marcia's name would be in those files, as his daughter.

Hichens had been able to access secret information systems at the Department of Defense and get names of military personnel who would be deployed for months out

258

to sea -- leaving their families prone to targeting and home break-ins.

Stocholm gave a call to Greer Thomson at the Internal Affairs Office of the C.I.A., who already knew there was a problem in the human resources department.

Private citizens had been contacting the agency for years, with FOIA requests trying to find out who was invading their privacy and threatening them with legal action on C.I.A. letter head stationery -- shortly after sending in job applications.

Now, after Stocholm's discovery of Vernon Hichens, there was enough evidence to charge Vernon with invasion of privacy and intent to commit fraud.

Greer called the Military Police at Ft. Belvoir, Virginia, and asked for two policemen to be on standby.

After Greer talked with the C.I.A.'s legal counsel, an order was signed by a judge to bring Vernon in for questioning and obtain his computer files.

The M.P.'s were called to escort Vernon to a holding cell at Ft. Belvoir. They arrived in two hours and handcuffed Vernon Hichens -- but not before Vernon had deleted the files of private citizens and victims of Zenithe organization from his computer files. He knew that phone call from Skooly would be trouble. Vernon had also managed to delete files of private citizens who had been covertly implanted with micro-chips and passive drugs.

That information was something that could get him killed.

When the M.P.'s showed up, Vernon quietly stuck out his hands for the cuffs – and said he wanted a lawyer.

49.

No such civil action would take place at Papua, New Guinea.

When word got back to Wilson Wallace and his commander in Hawaii about a terrorist control center being located in Bougainville, Wilson looked at his monitor to get a closer view of the island and its occupants. Everything looked pretty normal with rickshaws travelling dirt roads, women carrying babies on their backs in colored garbs, and men along waterways fishing.

But unknowingly to Wilson, a request had been made to a High Priest in Washington at The Religious Order of the Archaics -- an organization which had been established from the beginning of man's creation on earth and revelation of a holy God. The organization's by-laws mandated destruction of any invasive technological behavior and mind control center of any nation.

Hours later, a news channel would state a small earthquake had hit the island.

The High Priest was in command of all the activities in the world, inasmuch as terrorist organizations and politicians thought power came from within their own governments and genetic descent from family warlord mercenaries of the past, no entity could usurp the power of the High Priest and his religious order that ruled the people.

The rule of Caiaphas from the time of Jesus would stand and have authority.

With a Navy destroyer in the Indian Ocean bombing the bunker with two 5' gun shells during a training mission, the terrorist communication's center in the Highlands area would be obliterated.

The bombing would also be reported to be an accident -- from a training mission gone awry -- so diplomatic relations with the Papua Government could be appeased.

The way the U.S. looked at it, the bombing was doing the islanders a favor by loosening some of the dirt around old mine shafts where precious metals could be found. Causing a tsunami with a deep sea bomb off shore had been out the question – the bunker was too high in elevation and innocent people could be hurt with the flooding.

Marcia's targeting stopped immediately when a shell hit the bunker and a satellite link triangulating her with three cell phone towers was broken.

She sat in a daze – wondering if the earth had just stopped moving.

50.

Marcia was in her living room when her targeting stopped. There was no more music to her head, no pulling sensations around her body, and all her physical pains went away.

She got up from the couch walked straighter, without having to think about bumping into a wall. Her equilibrium, appetite, and will to live returned. She wanted to go out and tell someone but she knew Richie was working, so she called Naomi.

When Naomi answered the phone, Marcia could not stop talking about the freedom she was now experiencing.

Naomi said she also was feeling better.

Had the good people knocked out some antenna array that had been causing humans to be sick, disoriented, and confused, or was it just another feeling that would disappear in a couple of hours? Naomi was wondering.

"Maybe the perpetrators shut down the equipment for maintenance," Naomi suggested to Marcia. "Don't get excited," Naomi said. "I've been in this for years and it won't stop for long."

But Marcia didn't want to hear it. She was free and wanted to enjoy it. No more harassment, and she couldn't wait to tell Richie and Stronger.

But what if Naomi was right? Marcia thought. She would really look like a fool if she exclaimed something to be true that wasn't.

So she would have her own little party, and if Naomi wanted to join it, that was fine.

They planned to meet at a park in Denbigh and start off with ice cream. Then they'd go to the zoo and feed the animals, walk along the beach, and throw rocks in the water. They'd make flirtatious passes at men – if the men were wearing nice clothes.

Naomi said bad dressers in public had no respect.

"But what about carpenters, plumbers, and bricklayers who get dirty working?" Marcia asked.

"They're on the job honey. We're looking for business men. We got a lot of time to make up for."

Marcia smiled and thought about Richie, who had stuck his head out to help her. She knew who her business man was.

"Well, Rufus wears nice clothes," Marcia said.

"He does, doesn't he? You still have one of those cards?" Naomi asked.

"Sure. He'll be glad to hear from you, off duty of course."

Naomi took the card and smiled.

****

Made in the USA
Columbia, SC
24 July 2022